Like Wind Against Rock

ALSO BY NANCY KIM

Chinhominey's Secret

Like Wind Against Rock

a novel

NANCY KIM

Text copyright © 2021 by Nancy Kim
All rights reserved.

Published by Lake Union Publishing, Seattle

www.apub.com

Amazon, the Amazon logo, and Lake Union Publishing are trademarks of Amazon.com, Inc., or its affiliates.

ISBN-13: 9781542025461
ISBN-10: 154202546X

Cover design by Laywan Kwan

Printed in the United States of America

For my parents,
Yeun Soo and Mi Wha Kim

DEATH AND DIVORCE

CHAPTER ONE

I am sitting on Ahma's bed, waiting for her to come out of the bathroom and show me the new outfit that she is going to wear on her Friday-night date with a man she met at the gym. In houses all across America, mothers wait for daughters to emerge—ta-da!—from behind locked doors, transformed in shiny pastel dresses for proms, lacy confections for debutante balls, and fluffy white gowns for weddings. But in this house, it's the mother who dresses up and goes out while the daughter stays home and watches television in her sweats.

I glance at the clock on the nightstand. It is six forty-five.

"Ahma! You better hurry. He'll be here soon."

"It's okay! Man have to wait!" my mother yells from the bathroom. I sigh. Of course. *Man should wait for woman. Show woman more desirable. Not desperate.* Nope, no desperate women around here.

The bathroom door suddenly opens and Ahma bursts out like a superhero. Instead of a cape and tights, she is wearing a crinkled, sequin-encrusted top, skinny blue jeans, and silver stilettos. Her outfit makes me think of tropical fish. I hate to admit it, but she looks good—for a sixty-two-year-old. She also looks kind of bizarre, like a forty-year-old woman with the aura of a sixty-two-year-old woman rather than the other way around. She recently dyed the gray in her hair and had it cut in layers around her face. She is in the best shape I have ever seen her in, which is not too surprising since she has, for the first time in her life, started to exercise. She has even joined a gym, where she seems to be meeting every eligible bachelor in Orange County over the age of fifty.

Ahma stands in front of me, smiling widely. She is wearing red lipstick. When Appa was alive, she never wore lipstick. She also never wore tight blue jeans and spike heels.

"What you think?"

"Aren't you going to be cold?" I ask, although it's now July.

"Not cold! Jeans maybe too hot." She swishes her hips like a runway model.

"It . . . it looks kind of young." I want her to change into one of the outfits I am used to seeing her wear. Maybe the chocolate-brown velour sweats. Or the beige slacks with the white blouse. Or maybe just her comfortable flannel robe and fuzzy slippers.

"You just jealous," she says with a laugh. "I look good! Everybody say that! All the salesgirls say, 'Ah! You sixty-two? Can't believe it.'"

"Of course they'll say that. They're trying to sell you clothes."

"Nobody say that to *you* when you go shopping!"

My mother smiles and starts to comb her hair, which she has blown out.

The doorbell rings. Ahma searches for her purse.

"Stay there! I don't want him see you and think he some big deal!"

"I can't even meet your date?"

"What you think you are? My mother? Ha!"

In the past few months, my mother has started to speak to me solely in English, which I hate. Her English is surprisingly awful for someone who has lived in California for over forty years. But until the past year, she didn't have a single non-Korean friend. Now it seems that all her friends are single non-Koreans.

Ahma sits on the bed for a few minutes.

"What are you doing?"

"Man have to wait!" She takes several deep breaths. The doorbell rings again. And then again.

"Will you just go?"

Ahma calmly rises from the bed, purse in hand.

"Don't forget, lock door," she whispers, pointing to the doorknob.

I hear her open the door and then apologize for being late. I hear masculine exclamations of approval over her outfit. Immediate forgiveness of her tardiness. The front door closes. Morbid curiosity gets the better of me. I sneak downstairs and peer through the front curtains, just a peek. I see my mother with a tall, dark-haired stranger. I immediately notice two things about her date. He is much younger than she is, and he is Caucasian. Just like all her other dates. Ahma turns her head and glares menacingly *right at me*. I drop the curtain but then open it, just a sliver, in time to see them get into a powder-blue Porsche and drive away.

For three straight hours I watch reality shows and news programs. Crisis in the Mideast. Bank robbery in Santa Ana. A special on the precarious future of polar bears. I watch a majestic white creature drift away on an ice floe in the middle of the Arctic Ocean, floating away to certain death. I vow to buy less, drive less, and to reuse and recycle.

It is nearly eleven o'clock when I hear a car pull up into the driveway. I run to the upstairs hallway window and peer through the curtains. Ahma's date gets out of the Porsche and walks around to the passenger side. A true gentleman. She steps out like a princess. I run downstairs and settle myself on the sofa. The key turns in the lock, and the front door opens. I hear voices in the entryway. Laughter. Giggles! My mom is giggling like a schoolgirl. My stomach lurches. Suddenly there is silence as they seem to become aware of the mumbling from the television.

"Is somebody here?"

"My daughter."

I want to bolt from the sofa, but the only way out is the direction in which they are coming. I could hide behind the sofa, but who knows what might take place then. I stay rooted to my seat, my eyes fixated on the TV screen as though I am oblivious to their presence.

"Alice," my mother says. "You watch too much TV."

Ahma and her date are standing in the archway. He is politely smiling at me. He is tall, about six four. He has dark-brown hair with some gray around the temples. I hate to admit it, but he is handsome.

I hit the remote, and the screen goes dark.

"This is my daughter, Alice. This is Stephen."

I raise my butt from the couch so that I am half standing. "Hi."

Stephen gives me a half salute in response to my squat. "Hey there." He turns to Ahma. "I didn't know you lived with your daughter."

"She live with me," Ahma says. "Like old-fashion Korean."

"Just for a few weeks," I say. "My landlord decided to condo convert, so I moved out when my lease ended at the end of May."

"That's more than a few weeks," Stephen says. "It's already July."

"Who's counting?" I ask, but obviously he is. I turn to Ahma. "How was your . . . dinner?" I can't say the word *date* aloud, at least not in relation to any activity of my mother's.

"Delicious," my mother says. Stephen snorts, presumably at her lack of culinary sophistication.

"We dined at La Chemise," he says. He glances around the room as though he were thinking of buying the paint off the walls. La Chemise is a pricey French restaurant in Newport Beach. I'm supposed to be impressed, but instead I'm suspicious. It's a first date, not an anniversary dinner. What sort of payback is he expecting?

"Do you know why it's called 'La Chemise'?" Stephen asks, turning his discriminating shopper's gaze to me. Is he always this condescending?

"Because a meal there will cost you the shirt off your back?"

Stephen acts like he doesn't hear me. "It used to be a shirt factory, if you can believe it. But the feds closed it down and sent all the little ladies back to China."

"You want something drink?" my mother asks him, her eyes and mouth open with exaggerated hospitality.

"Hmmm . . ." Stephen glances over at me. I glare at him with my eyes but smile like a geisha with my lips. "I think we should call it a night."

"Good idea," my mother says, her brows furrowed with under-standing. "Have to surgery tomorrow early."

"Exactly," he says with a nod. He turns to me. "Nice to meet you." His eyes are round with insincerity.

"Nice to meet you."

My mother walks him to the door. I'm not sure, but I think I hear the quick, smacking sound of lips on flesh, and I cringe.

I turn the television back on. My mother sits on the couch next to me.

"What you think?" she asks.

"Gasoline's going through the roof. Better fill up your tank tomor-row. They're expecting another hike."

"Not gas. Stephen. Handsome, yes?"

"I guess. He's kind of young for you."

"More energy!" She raises her arms in the air like she's just won the Tour de France.

"More energy for what? To go disco dancing?"

"Nobody disco anymore." Ahma gives me a look of pity. "We play squash."

"Squash? When did you take up squash?"

"Next weekend. Stephen going to teach me."

I pick up the remote and change the channel. "See? I told you. Everyone says gas prices will rise this weekend."

"You watch too much junk TV."

"Yeah, well, I didn't have a hot date to keep me busy."

Ahma gives me a funny look, nose slightly wrinkled, eyes squinted. It's the same look she gives me when I eat too much kimchi and forget to floss.

"You think he should be your date."

"No, I don't."

"It's normal. I have date. Stephen is a handsome and your same age. He drive expensive car."

"I don't care about that."

7

One side of her mouth curves skeptically.

"Your old mama get hot dude."

"Will you quit talking like that? Don't say 'dude'!"

"I even take your cool talk."

"It's not cool to say 'dude.' You're not a . . . surfer!"

"Stephen knows surf."

"Good for Stephen."

"He say he show me how."

"You can't do that."

"Why not? I have good shape. Everyone say so." She smooths her hands against her waist and straightens her spine.

"I know. They can't believe how old you are."

"Grandma age." She is halfway up the stairs when she leans her head over the railing and shares, "Stephen like jeans."

I roll my eyes. I bet he does.

Ahma wasn't always such a desperate housewife. When I was growing up, the battles over clothing concerned my skimpy outfits. She wore shapeless shift dresses or khaki slacks and white polo shirts. She was big on designer handbags, but they were usually knockoffs. After Appa died in April, she underwent some kind of transformation and changed everything—the way she looked, her friends, the way she talked. I expected a mourning period. Appa was her life, or at least that's what I'd thought.

~

A couple of weeks after my father died, I found two men hooking his beige Audi to a tow truck.

"What's going on?" I asked my mother, who stood in the doorway with a blank expression. "Why are they taking Appa's car?"

"I don't want keep your daddy car."

"And what's all that?" There were four stuffed garbage bags at the curb.

"Junk." She turned and walked into the house. I followed her. Inside, she busied herself making tea, a convenient way to avoid eye contact.

"He had that car for years. How do you know that I don't want it?"

"No reason keep old car. You have car. Old car too expensive maintenance."

Of course she was right, but I couldn't understand her efficiency in trashing his things. Isn't there a denial period to mourning? Isn't it supposed to take months, even years, to accept the death of a loved one?

My parents seemed to have had an understanding about how their marriage would work. My mother would belong to the family and be the witness to my life. She was the one who kept the household functioning, the one who was there when I got home from school. She was the one who made dinner every night, the one who made the doctor's appointments and bought the toothpaste and toilet paper. My father stood at the periphery of our family, both a guard and an honored guest. He ventured out into the world in the mornings and returned in the evenings. He was the one who ensured we were able to live in a nice house in a good neighborhood. He was the one who made sure we were safe in the world. I always thought she was grateful to him for this, for being a good provider, for being dependable. He may have been reserved, but he was never cruel or unkind. Now that he was dead—her husband of over forty years!—I expected Ahma to show some emotion. But she didn't seem to miss him. His death seemed to have left no emptiness in her heart.

The teakettle screamed. She started to pour the water into the teapot. She cursed and dropped the kettle onto the kitchen floor. I rushed over and thrust her hand under the kitchen faucet.

"It's okay!" she yelled, trying to take back her hand. I held on to her wrist and forced her fingers to stay under the running water. They were red, and their undersides were already starting to rise into welts. I turned to look at her. Up close, I could see that her entire face was swollen and blotchy. She averted her eyes, as though I had caught her doing something shameful.

I picked up the teakettle, wiped the spill, and then poured hot water into the teapot. While the tea steeped, we each waited for the other to say something.

My father's death was sudden and unexpected. The doctor said it was stress-induced cardiomyopathy, which means that his heart stopped working. I had no idea that he'd had problems with his heart, or that he had been experiencing unusual stress. Almost as sudden as my father's heart failure was my mother's transformation from grieving widow to swinging single. It was as if she only allotted herself a couple of weeks to mourn and then, by sheer force of will, moved to the next chapter of her life. She purged Appa's belongings as though she were meeting a deadline. What was more aggravating was that she wouldn't let me help, telling me that I would get in the way. Those four garbage bags I had seen outside were the last remnants of my father's life.

"What if there's something in those bags that I want to keep?" I asked.

"Just junk."

"Maybe to you, but I might not think so."

"Anything good, I leave for you."

And she had left a pile for me. Fancy fountain pens, gold cuff links, and a mound of cashmere sweaters and scarves—all things that had objective monetary value but no sentimental value. The rest she had stuffed into the four extra-strength garbage bags and dragged to the curb for trash pickup.

"I'm going to just go through them and see—"

"*No!*" she said, her voice suddenly sharp. It was a tone she didn't use often, and it typically would have made me drop the subject. But I was upset, too.

"What if you missed something? What if there's something that I want to keep?"

She turned to me, one hand on her hip, her face taut, as though it were pulled tight by a string. "What? What you looking for?"

"I don't know." But I did know. I was looking for memories, something to remember him by. Something that would reveal how much my father loved me. He had never been very expressive, and even when he was home, he was never really present. What did I hope to find? Homemade cards that he had saved from me, his only daughter? Crayon drawings from kindergarten? Things that he'd accepted with barely a nod of acknowledgment, often not even that—maybe they'd meant more to him than he'd let on?

Ahma seemed to know, and her expression softened as though the string had been released. "We have picture. Lots of picture."

I nodded.

"He already tell you everything when he was alive. If he don't tell you . . . you don't need to know."

She was right, the way she was always right. But still, I was his daughter. Shouldn't I have the right to say goodbye, in some way? But no, she was his wife, his widow, and my mother. She had veto power, and she used it. I felt the unfairness as acutely as I did when I was a child and had no choice but to go to bed, brush my teeth, clean my room, wear the ugly raincoat.

That evening, I pulled out of her driveway and waved goodbye to Ahma, who stood on the front stoop, solemnly waving back. The stuffed garbage bags beckoned to me from the curbside like four dumpy, forlorn hitchhikers. I drove the twenty minutes to my apartment, brushed my teeth, and changed into my pajamas. I climbed into bed, turned out the light, and stared at the inside of my eyelids for a few hours. I practiced the body-relaxation technique that always worked in yoga class. I focused on relaxing my toes, then my calves, then my knees, and so on, all the way up my body. By the time I got to my eyebrows, I was wide awake and out the door, car keys clutched in my fist.

With each mile, I grew more anxious. What if the garbage collectors had already come by? But I knew it was still too early. The sky was black, even the stars had gone to sleep. What if someone else had picked up the bags? I pressed my bare foot down on the accelerator. I turned the corner onto Bernardo Lane, switched off my headlights, and stopped in front of the house where my mother now lived alone. The four bags waited, their bellies sagging like men who had given up hope. I opened the trunk of my car. Was it stealing if they were being discarded? Was it theft if they had once belonged to my father? I felt like a crook, because no matter what it was called, it was wrong. I was directly disobeying my mother's wishes, even though she had no right to make decisions for me, even though I had a right to mourn. I wanted to dig through my father's belongings and decide for myself what to keep, what to toss. The truth was, I didn't want to toss a single thing. The bags were heavy. I wondered how Ahma had dragged them to the curb without ripping them. My pajama T-shirt was damp with sweat by the time I got back into the car and drove away.

Feeling like a murderer with a body to hide, I dragged one bag a few feet and then the next, continuing that way until I had all four bags in the elevator. The lobby was empty, and I wanted to hurry and get to the safety of my apartment before anyone could see me. I didn't want to answer any questions. I needed no witnesses to this act of filial disloyalty. Ahma shouldn't have put me in this situation anyway. What was the big deal? It wasn't like I was stealing anything from her. It would have all ended up in the trash anyway. So what was the harm?

But I knew. Even without knowing what it was, I was looking for something that she did not want me to find. I know Ahma too well. She is a cheapskate, a saver. She keeps things because she doesn't like to spend money unnecessarily and because she doesn't want to be punished for wasting God's resources. With my mother, superstition, religion, and conservation are inextricably bound. Her God doesn't demand prayers before meals or attendance at church but damns those who waste rice and electricity. Ahma should have recycled Appa's belongings. Instead, she seemed to want to remove all trace of his existence by sending his belongings to the dump. She was upset, maybe even angry, and I suspected that something in those four bloated plastic bags would explain why.

I loosened the mouth of the first bag. Then the second and the third. Old slacks and books and stained shirts freed themselves and polluted my small apartment with the smell of mothballs, dust, and the stale scent of my father's aftershave. In the fourth bag was more junk—old pens and papers and toiletries and a large yellow envelope. I bent the metal clasp to open the envelope and peered inside. A soft-cover notebook. A journal of some sort, written in my father's handwriting. The date of each entry was written in the top-right-hand corner of the pages, which was the only thing I could decipher. The rest of the notebook was written in hangul, Korean characters. This was what I was looking for. I didn't know what it meant, but I knew it was important.

CHAPTER TWO

After the funeral, Ahma joined a gym, lost ten pounds, got a new haircut, and found a new job. I, on the other hand, gained ten pounds and lost a husband. Louis had filed for divorce.

Louis and I had already been separated for a year by that time. I was living in a one-bedroom apartment near our old place. It wasn't far from my parents, although I hadn't told them that my marriage was falling apart and that I had moved out. They were old fashioned, and to them, a separation would have been shameful, although not as shameful as divorce. Secretly, I hoped that Louis and I could continue the way we were, living apart but legally married. There was no reason to go through with all that paperwork, was there? We had been together so long, and divorce was so final. We still liked each other. Louis knew what a big deal our separation would be for my parents, and he was a sport about it. He even came with me to dinner at my parents' house occasionally, just to keep up the charade. When I told him that my father had died, he said he would pick me up and we would go to the funeral together. I think I'll always love him for that.

After the funeral, Louis drove me to my apartment. We sat in the car together. I felt it then, his longing to comfort me, to soothe me and hold me as I cried. But I just couldn't. Instead, I thanked him for driving and gave him a peck on the cheek. I ran up to my apartment, closed the door, and cried for everything I had lost.

That night, some line was crossed. We both knew that we couldn't go back to the way things were, but only Louis could admit it. Two weeks later, he came by to talk, but my heart wasn't in it. Then he told me that he was filing for divorce. His timing could have been better, given that my father had just died. But if he hadn't done it then, we might have continued the way we had been for another decade. Maybe my dad's sudden death made him realize that we were all running out of time.

I always sensed that my parents weren't crazy about Louis, but he was so helpful that they didn't have the heart to criticize him. He stopped by my parents' house to fix their clogged sinks, trim tree branches—he even retiled their bathroom floor. They treated him like the son they never had. It wasn't long before we adapted, acting like brother and sister instead of lovers. We trained ourselves to keep our feelings for each other in check when we were with my parents and, because we spent so much time with them, what had started as an act became reality for us. We started to feel uncomfortable when we were alone together, in our rented house with no distracting pets and no demanding kids. What we felt when it was just the two of us wasn't the awkwardness of strangers but the lonely quiet of a party after the guests have departed.

It was already too late by the time we got married. Maybe passion naturally dissipates after a certain period of time for all couples. I assumed with my parents it was just a cultural difference, but maybe time does that to all married couples. Louis and I had been together since our freshman year of college—nearly twelve years—before we decided to get married. But our marriage only lasted five years. Maybe because we'd taken each other for granted for so long, marriage couldn't consecrate our mundane relationship and transform it into something precious. We had hoped it would infuse our love with passion. We wanted to feel like hormone-charged adolescents. We wanted to be the kind of newlyweds who couldn't wait to rip off each other's clothes on our wedding night. Our minds were in sync, but our bodies just weren't that into it. Whoever said that the brain is the largest erogenous zone has never been in a long-term relationship. We gossiped about the guests, groaned over the toasts, raved over the food. Then we brushed our teeth, flossed, and took off our clothes. He rolled on top of me, we did our thing, and then we pulled our bodies apart and kissed. "That was nice," he said. I nodded. We held hands and fell asleep.

Louis and I first met at the Chancellor's Ball for incoming students. His friends dared him to ask me to dance. "Please don't laugh in my face," he pleaded, his face stiff with embarrassment, his mouth like a ventriloquist's, barely moving.

I glanced over at the group of guys, who were too obviously trying to be nonchalant, and asked, "A bet?"

He nodded.

"Are they betting I'll say yes or no?"

"Definitely no."

"If I say yes, what's in it for you?"

He held my eyes and said, "A case of Heineken. And if I'm lucky, maybe your phone number?"

We drank the beer that night with his friends.

Although he didn't believe it, Louis was the first boy I ever slept with. "But you're so hot," he murmured in my ear as he slipped his hands underneath my paisley-print blouse. "Your dad must have a shotgun." In truth, it was Ahma, not Appa, who kept me from dating throughout most of high school. With the exception of the Homecoming Dance and prom my senior year, I spent most of my Saturday nights during high school watching television with her while Appa worked late or went out with his friends. I always got a weekend synopsis from my best friend, Janine, who had no curfew and lots more fun.

I never actually told my parents that I was dating Louis. They met him for the first time at college graduation, after we had been dating for almost four years.

"This is Louis," I said.

My father nodded as his eyes scanned the crowd for something more interesting. My mother smiled and extended her hand.

"Nice to meet you, Loudeese," she said.

About a year ago, Louis started to talk about things that didn't interest me, like life and legacies, ambitions and desires. When he started to rant and rave about the overpriced real estate market or the lack of affordable health care, a coffee cup or a bottle of beer in his hand, I wanted to flee the room. It wasn't what he was saying but what it meant. He was looking to the future, and I wasn't ready. We started to do something that we almost never did. We fought. At least it was a version of fighting, with him yelling at me and me looking away and trying not to get mad, trying not to engage him in an argument. It was a communication style I had learned from my parents, who never argued or kissed in my presence. It's what he eventually threw in my face, my "disengagement" from our relationship. I tried to avoid a squabble and ended up with a divorce.

California law has a six-month waiting period, so our divorce won't be final until mid-October, another three months. After we separated last year, Louis traveled around the world for six weeks. When he returned, he called to tell me that he was training to be a financial analyst. I laughed when I heard this.

"You must be the only person on the planet who goes soul-searching in India and discovers his inner capitalist."

"It was time to start thinking about the future."

"So you decided to be a stockbroker?"

"It's a financial-services company, not a brokerage. Anyway, it's practical. Did you think I would be a slacker my entire life?"

That stung. Maybe he hadn't meant to take a dig at me, but we both knew that I was not living up to my potential by working as a part-time bookkeeper. I stared at the peeling paint on the bedroom walls. For the first time, I noticed that the white walls had gradually faded and aged until they were now a sickly yellow.

"Do you like it?"

"Yeah, I do. It makes me feel like I have a purpose in life."

I didn't tell him that I thought it was pathetic that his purpose in life was to teach people what to do with their money. It was even more pathetic that our marriage had failed to give him the purpose that the stock market now did.

I've always considered Louis to be my first boyfriend, although I guess technically, he may not have been. I went to two dances with Jim during my senior year in high school. Jim was on the football team and scored the most touchdowns in the history of Green Hills High. But I never saw him play, since I never went to any football games. I didn't think he was particularly smart or funny, but he liked me for some reason, and that was reason enough for me to say yes when he asked me to the Homecoming Dance. If I am completely honest with myself, maybe I was flattered that I'd bested the blonde cheerleaders who suddenly seemed to notice that I existed. We didn't really date, since Ahma didn't allow me to go out at night unless it was a special occasion. It was a bit of a mystery why he chose to ask me to the two biggest dances of the year, since I didn't offer him much. I allowed him only a quick peck on the cheek after the Homecoming Dance, and a quick peck on the lips after the senior prom.

But I learned something about Jim and the nature of attraction at a party that took place the summer after graduation. Ahma let me go after Janine begged her, promising to have me home before midnight. The party was supposed to be a big one, since Megan, the girl who was hosting it, had an older sister who went to Saint Vincent's, the nearby Catholic high school. The girls who went to Saint Vincent's had a reputation for being wild, and that ensured a large turnout from the Green Hills boys.

I was mildly surprised to see friends from school brazenly drinking beer from bottles and pulling on joints. Of course I knew that this happened, but it was one thing to hear about what happened at parties and another to actually experience it. Jim was at the party, standing in the kitchen with his best friends, Walter and Greg. They were chatting up a few girls from Saint Vincent's. The girls wore high heels, with tight jeans and halter tops. Jim seemed to have a particular interest in a girl with waist-length black hair and an olive complexion. She was the only other Asian at the party. I felt the color rush to my cheeks. All this time, I had thought that Jim liked *me*, when it turned out that he just liked Asian girls. Janine glanced over at me with a stricken expression, and I was touched by her empathy. My humiliation didn't end there. Later, after a lot of people had left, and long after the time Janine had promised my mother she would have me home, we were sitting on the couch in the living room when Walter came storming into the room with an excited grin. "Jim is doing it with that Chinese girl upstairs!" The room fell silent and everyone looked at me. I stared at the table and took a sip of the cola I had been nursing all evening. Then we heard it. A rhythmic thumping sound and breathless *yeah, baby*s. Janine sprang from the couch and raced upstairs. We could hear her pounding on the door, screaming profanities at Jim and the "slut" with no shame who had so easily replaced me.

Louis was the polar opposite of Jim, which may be why it wasn't difficult for me to trust him. While I let Jim kiss me only twice, I never felt like I needed to draw boundaries so firmly with Louis. He was sensitive to ambiguities, able to tolerate indecision. Louis wanted to be a working musician, and he rationalized that even if he didn't make it big, at least he'd be doing what he loved. Making money didn't matter the way making music did. He picked up some web-design work because we still had to eat and pay the rent. But I think that no matter what he said—all that garbage about doing what he loved and not trying to be a rock star—he *did* think he was going to make it. Maybe he wouldn't be the next Bono, but he thought that he could make a decent living somehow if he kept at it long enough.

The years passed, and one by one, our friends from college traded in their instruments and paintbrushes for luxury cars and mortgages. But not us, and it was okay for a while. It didn't feel like we were slackers. We were romantics, idealists. They were sellouts, but not us. It doesn't feel that way anymore, now that Louis has abandoned his dream, and me.

My relationship with my soon-to-be ex-husband is pleasant now, but I can't say that we are best friends. We don't see each other much, which is less painful than I would have thought if I had ever thought about it when we were together. Now, when we talk, it's a brief phone conversation about the logistics of dissolution, legal paperwork, items to return, sorting bits of this and that from our nearly two decades together. The conversation is stilted, and we are as polite as strangers.

He's called me tonight to tell me that he found my social security card in one of his coat pockets. I'm not sure how it ended up there, but I'm not surprised. Our lives were so intertwined that it will be a while before we are really separated. I can still smell his scent when I pull on a sweater that I haven't worn in a while, and he undoubtedly still finds long black strands of my hair on his shirts.

"Are things still good at work?" I ask.

"Yeah. Great."

"I'm glad to hear that."

In the silence, I can visualize his annoyed expression. If we were still living together, he would taunt, "Why don't you tell me what you *really* think?" He might have even called me an emotional coward. But there is no point anymore.

"Have you found a new place yet?" I ask. The last time we spoke, Louis told me that he was sick of renting, that he was thinking of buying.

"Yeah, sort of," he says, and then he stops. In his pause, I realize that he is seeing someone else. It's been well over a year since we separated, so I shouldn't be surprised. Still, I pray he won't say anything more so that we can go on pretending. I need to, even if he doesn't.

"How is your mom?" he finally asks, and I think of how decent he is, how kind. The failure of our marriage is nobody's fault.

"Fine."

"Good. Tell her I say hello."

CHAPTER THREE

At the beginning of May, my landlord gave me notice that he was planning to convert the apartment building into condominiums. He said that I could stay until construction started, on a month-to-month basis, and he offered to let me purchase one of the units at an astronomical price. My mother made me a better offer.

"You stay with me," she said. "House is too big now. You can save money."

I knew her offer meant not only that I could stay rent-free but that I wouldn't have to pay a dime in expenses, including groceries. This was a financial lifeline. Paying rent had been a huge strain on my budget. But I also knew that when Ahma said, "You stay with me," she meant me and Louis. She thought we were still living together. I hadn't yet told her about the separation. When she suggested that Louis and I could take the more spacious master bedroom and she would take my old room, I had to come clean. Sort of.

"It's just a break. For a little while," I lied.

"No divorce," she said. It was not a question but a statement in need of confirmation.

"No, not a divorce."

"Okay," she said, then added, "I keep master bedroom."

I know I'll have to tell her someday, but I can't do it now. It's too soon, for both of us. My mom is the only one left for me, as I am for her.

It would be different if I had a sibling, someone with whom I could share the experience of being in a family, *our* family. Maybe then I wouldn't feel so alone.

I remember coming home from school one day—I must have been about seven or eight—tired of being the only one of my friends without a sibling. I wanted someone who would follow me around and play with me whenever I wanted. I imagined us opening presents together on Christmas morning and sitting in the back seat during long car rides.

"I want a baby brother or sister—everyone else has one."

Ahma didn't say anything. She just looked at me, and her expression was so sad that I knew I had said something wrong. But I was a kid, so I persisted.

"Please. Just one. I want a baby to play with."

"Me too," she finally said and turned her head.

Her answer made no sense. If she wanted a baby, too, then why couldn't we have one? But even at that young age, I knew I shouldn't ask. Even then, I knew that some things were best left unspoken.

On the first day of June, I moved into my old bedroom. It was easier to move this time, since I had been in my apartment less than a year and had already done an extensive purge of my belongings. Yet I still had more to discard, since I was moving from a one-bedroom apartment to one bedroom. This was further evidence that I was regressing, my life contracting instead of expanding. All my possessions had to fit into my car. There was no need to take my dented cookware or threadbare linens. They were from my married life, old and cheap, and not worth the storage space. Once I found a new place, I would buy nice new things, start over for real this time.

But that would all be in the perfect future. In the messy present, I had no money, and a housewares-shopping trip to Target was out of the question. Anyway, Ahma already had housewares and linens, so I took only what I needed and the things I cared about the most. That included my father's belongings, of course—the old cashmere sweaters that Ahma had saved for me, and his notebook, which I had saved from her.

It's been a month now since I moved in with Ahma, and I'm more or less settled. I keep the yellow envelope hidden at the back of the closet in my childhood bedroom. I flip through the pages every now and then, looking at my father's neat handwriting. It is a plain composition notebook. I recently spent some time researching translation services online. Not many of them translate Korean to English, and the few that I found were expensive and seemed sketchy, their websites full of typos and weird grammar. I don't feel comfortable sending my father's notebook to a stranger to translate without knowing what it says, and I won't know what it says without sending it to a stranger to translate. Still, I am curious.

I have a feeling it is something personal. A diary, perhaps? But my father wasn't the type to keep a diary, and I never saw him write in one. I don't remember ever seeing him write anything other than a check. My mom usually scrawled out all the birthday cards when I was young, signing them very formally, "Your Loving Mother and Father."

Maybe it was a practice he developed after I went away to college. But if it is his diary, then why would Ahma throw it away? Is she that unsentimental? Doesn't she miss him at all?

~

"There are supposed to be seven stages to death," I tell Janine. "Apparently nobody told my mom."

We're in a booth at El Toreador, Janine's favorite restaurant, locally famous for its strong margaritas and spicy salsa. The food is greasy and too salty, but nobody comes to eat anyway. Like Janine, they all come for the margaritas.

Janine doesn't think Ahma's rapid recovery is all that shocking.

"They say that it's harder for people to get over a divorce than the death of a spouse," she tells me before licking the salt off her glass. She reminds me of a cat cleaning itself. She is wearing a tight red pencil skirt and a black fuzzy short-sleeve sweater, even though it is nearly eighty degrees. She has pulled her hair into a high ponytail and is wearing her tortoise-frame glasses. It's her "sexy librarian" look, which means that if I'm not careful, she will be dancing on tabletops tonight. Janine's idea of having fun is the same as it was when she was in college.

After graduation, I went to UC Irvine, primarily because it was close enough for me to come home whenever I wanted. Janine, who had a lower GPA but a greater sense of adventure, ended up tending bar at a ski resort in Colorado for a year, ran out of money, and then returned home to get her degree at the community college. When I was married, we saw each other occasionally, but not as much as we do now. When I told her that Louis and I were getting a divorce, she sounded nearly gleeful, but not because she was malicious or didn't like him. Her friends, like my own, had all gotten married and started families. She saw social possibility in my marital disaster.

"I guess I always hoped that my parents were really crazy about each other deep down and that they were just hiding all that passion for my sake."

"Count yourself lucky. Believe me, it's no fun having parents so passionate about each other you think they're going to either have sex in front of you or kill each other."

Janine's parents divorced when we were in high school.

"At least they felt something for each other."

"Passion is no guarantee that the marriage is going to last. Or that it will keep someone's dick in his pants."

She's talking about her own father now, who left her mother for his secretary. Such a cliché.

"Still, it's kind of surprising," I say. "I thought it would take her longer than this to get back on her feet. I never imagined she would start dating at all, and so soon?"

"Your mom doesn't have to hold out hope that her husband's coming back. He's gone forever. You, on the other hand . . ." She sticks a chip into the salsa and stuffs it into her red-rimmed mouth. She flaps her hands. "Yeow! That's really hot."

"We've been here dozens of times. You know the salsa is spicy."

Janine stuffs another chip doused in salsa into her mouth. "Yahem, I know." She polishes off her margarita and motions the waiter for a refill. She fans her mouth. "This salsa! It's going to kill me!"

She grabs my margarita and takes a chug and then picks up another chip. "These are just so good—I can't stop eating them!" Her eyes are watering, but she scoops more salsa onto her chip. She reaches again for my margarita. "You can have mine when it gets here," she gasps. She grabs another chip.

This happens every time we come here. Chip, salsa, margarita, chip, salsa, margarita . . . it's a vicious cycle. Next, she's going to want to go to a lousy club and rub up against some musician while I sit by myself in a corner booth sipping ice water. Is this what the next ten years of my life look like?

"Are you hungry?" she asks. "I'm not really hungry."

"You just had two baskets of chips and two margaritas . . ."

The waiter places another drink in front of her. She raises it in a toast. "To finding you a new man!"

She says this so loudly that the couple at the next table glances over at us and smirks smugly. I know how they feel. I used to be just like them.

"I'm not looking for a new man," I hiss.

"Did you forget about Friendship Rule Number One?"

She is referring to the rules that we made up when we were in middle school. We called them the "Rules of Friendship," which would govern our friendship for life. We weren't supposed to keep secrets from each other (Rule #1), and we had to tell each other if we had a crush on someone (Rule #2, which was actually an application of Rule #1 but important enough to merit its own rule), and if one of our crushes showed that he liked the other one (by asking that girl to dance, although it included other things, like giving the girl a valentine), then that girl had to get permission from the other girl before accepting the dance or the valentine (Rule #3). Of course we added to our Rules of Friendship as the years passed so that they included cheating (or not) on tests (Rule #12), which girls we could invite to sleepovers (Rule #6), and whether we (meaning Janine, because I didn't go out) should drink beer at parties in high school (Rule #16) and, if so, how many we should drink (Rule #17).

"I'm telling the truth. I'm not looking for a new relationship," I say.

"Oh, come on, raise your glass," she says.

"There's nothing in it."

"It's symbolic," she says.

I lift my empty goblet and clink it against hers. Her drink sloshes onto her fingers, and she laughs and takes a sip.

"I think you have a drinking problem."

"That's only because I'm on a diet," she says. "I can drink anything I want, as long as I *eat* only nine hundred calories," she says.

"That's crazy! Where did you hear about this diet?"

"On the internet."

Ninety minutes later, I am sitting by myself at the back of the Slo Club while Janine canoodles some part-time saxophonist while swaying to moody lounge tunes. I am trying not to make eye contact with anyone for fear that I might be approached—which, so far, is not a huge problem. I should have done this right after high school, when I might have thought it was fun. Instead, I went from sitting on the couch watching television with Ahma to sitting on the couch watching television with Louis. I'm too old now to be barhopping with Janine. This is not progress.

Janine's face suddenly appears in front of mine. "Isn't this more exciting than watching TV?" Her mascara is smudged, and her breath smells of alcohol. Mr. Sax takes the stage and dedicates the next set to "that beautiful brunette in the corner." Janine beams like a schoolgirl. Only she's not. We're not.

26

CHAPTER FOUR

The commute to work takes fifteen minutes longer from Ahma's house. Even though I've been here over a month now, I still underestimate the extra time it takes being in a new location, finding my clothes, chatting with my mom, eating breakfast. I used to just grab a latte on the way to work, but Ahma insists I sit down and eat something. This morning, she has made me scrambled eggs with a mound of steaming rice. I'm not really hungry, but my plate is waiting for me like a rebuke. I am living, rent-free, in her house. What right do I have to refuse a nutritious meal? Ahma doesn't even make me wash my plate, insisting that she'll do it—I better hurry or I'll be late.

I *am* thirty minutes late to Harry Gee, my first client, but he merely smiles and waves as he talks on the phone. Harry owns a discount men's clothing store that has been around for years. I got this gig when his old accountant died. I spend Monday, Wednesday, and Friday mornings in Long Beach taking care of Harry's books and those afternoons in Anaheim at the office of Randolph Johnson, a retired and wealthy real estate investor, who has a whole team of financial advisers but needs me to do basic bookkeeping. On Tuesdays and Thursdays I drive forty minutes to the Restin Public Library as an accounting "floater" working with Special Collections. My job was created from a public-private initiative passed by voters in the last election. Restin is like that—wealthy but generous.

I don't know exactly how I became a bookkeeper, except that I've always been pretty good with numbers. When I was in elementary school, they put me in these special genius classes where I was the only girl. The boys all wore Coke-bottle glasses and watched *Star Trek*. My eyesight was perfect, and I couldn't keep my fingers together in a Vulcan greeting to save my life, yet I was still the math and chess champion of Westfield Elementary. But being the best at math is different than, say, being the best at cartwheels or jumping rope. While the other genius boys played together, they pretty much ignored me. The girls didn't want anything to do with me. I didn't get invited to birthday parties and sleepovers and stood around by myself during recess and lunch. Being the budding genius that I was, I devised a solution. I started to say "I dunno" to questions when I knew the answers and, on the timed exams that we took every few weeks, I counted to thirty before filling in each bubble on the answer sheet so that I never completed them. I sat on my hands so that I wouldn't wave them around wildly in response to questions that hung heavily in the air. It worked. By the time I reached sixth grade, I was kicked out of the genius class and put in with the normal kids. I think everyone was relieved when that happened. Appa ruffled my hair and said, "The tallest rice stalk always gets cut down." Ahma expressed hope that I might actually get married now that I wasn't smarter than every boy in my class, as though I might actually consider marrying one of them at the ripe old age of eleven. My bearded Trekkie teacher, Mr. Richardson, reassured me that I was still pretty smart, for a girl. He tried to convince me that the early promise I'd shown was simply a developmental fluke, like a growth spurt. He told me that there was something about the female brain that made it impossible for girls to be as good as boys in math and science. "Look at all the famous scientists and inventors. Newton. Einstein. Salk. All men." I opened my mouth to offer up Curie but remembered that he was merely falling into the trap that I had set, and instead swallowed hard. "Don't feel bad," he said. "You'll do all right in life." I wonder what would have happened if I *had* said the words *Marie Curie*, or had parents who expected more from me, or if I had simply believed that being invited to sleepovers wasn't as important as finding an algorithm that would unlock the mysteries of the universe.

Now, I balance books by default, because it's something I can do without really trying. I drive around from client to client with my laptop and flash drive, clicking my mouse and counting their money. The work is not awful but doesn't thrill me. It's a living, but is it a life?

Sometimes I daydream about enrolling in a graduate program in economics. I even went so far as to take the GRE and did much better than I expected. But I couldn't figure out what to write in the essays, and I never felt like filling out the applications. Would having a PhD really make a difference? Anyway, the program is seven long years. I would be too old when I finished, only a few years shy of fifty. Louis used to tell me that I never wanted anything enough. I wondered why he thought that was such a bad thing, given the luck he'd had as a musician.

It's funny that Louis is working in financial services, since he was always so awful with our finances. I was the numbers person in our relationship. I was the one who balanced our checkbook and paid the bills. He was the one who composed music and couldn't remember what day it was—the ninth? Or the tenth? No, Louis, it's the eleventh. Time flies when you play gigs at night and freelance as a web designer. Now he wants to work market hours. I'm not sure why the idea bothers me so much. Probably because he's moving on, and I feel left behind. The train has left the station with Louis on it, and I haven't even climbed onto the platform.

The thing that gets to me is that I didn't plan this. It wasn't like I made the choice to be a bookkeeper for the rest of my life, or to rent and not own, or to be childless and divorced at the age of thirty-nine. That's the problem. If, at any point in my life, someone had forced me to make a *decision*, I might have chosen something else. At least, that's what I like to think.

Ahma isn't home when I return from work. It is only six o'clock, and I am starving. I open the refrigerator door, only to discover that there isn't much to eat. Some pickled beets, preserved radishes, some kind of marinated root. Anchovies made sticky sweet with sugar and soy sauce.

Hardly any fresh fruits or vegetables. I didn't think about the need for grocery shopping, just as I had never thought about it before when I was a kid and took for granted that Ahma would have dinner ready. I have been living at her house since June, and she has made us dinner almost every night, except for the weekends. Without being entirely conscious of it, I was expecting her to have dinner waiting again tonight, which is of course ridiculous, given her work schedule. After Appa died, she got a job working at a real estate agency, driving around rich Koreans looking to buy in the best neighborhoods. She's apparently pretty good at it. She's in escrow on her third house. She has some arrangement with her agency, since she isn't a licensed broker yet, so she doesn't get the standard broker's commission. Still, the houses are north of a million, so whatever she gets, she's definitely making more than I am now.

I can understand her wanting to get a job after Appa's death, but I am surprised by her gung-ho attitude. She hustles as though she needs the money, but Appa was a dentist with a busy practice, and the house is paid for. She rushes around as though she's in a hurry to catch up on the life that she missed. But life with Appa wasn't so bad, was it? My parents never had a passionate marriage, and I always had the feeling that it was my father's fault. When I think about them together, she's leaning toward him, and he's always pulling away. I remember all the times she offered him something to eat—"Try this"—and how he would refuse, shaking his head and turning away. How many times did she brush something off his shirt or fix his tie, only to have him move away annoyed and brush or fix it himself? I didn't think much about it at the time—it was just the way they were. But now I wonder—what would it be like to spend so many years with someone who recoiled whenever you tried to get close?

I had always assumed that my parents loved each other, even if they didn't hug and kiss each other in front of me. I figured that was just the way they *were* and didn't question it, just like I didn't question why it was always Ahma who went to parent-teacher conferences, even though Appa was the one who could communicate in English more effectively. They had their respective roles. Ahma's life revolved around our family and our needs, like the moon revolves around the earth, and Appa was the sun, the distant yet essential center of our universe. At least, that's what I always thought. But now that he's dead, I'm no longer so sure. Rather than going dark and frozen, Ahma's world seems to be thawing, becoming vibrantly alive. Which makes me wonder—did my parents stay together for my sake? I recall a conversation I had with my mother when I was in tenth grade, after Janine's parents had split up. My mom acted like they had committed murder.

"Why divorce? What about your friend?"

Ahma's always referred to Janine as "my friend," even though she's been my best friend since seventh grade.

"She's going to live with her mom and visit her dad every other weekend. And holidays."

"So selfish! Not good for children."

"Janine's almost sixteen. Her brother is twelve."

"Why divorce?"

"Her dad was having an affair."

I thought that I had dropped a bomb, but my mom hardly blinked. "How does she know?"

"I don't know."

"Then not sure."

"They probably didn't want to give their kids the gory details."

"No need to divorce because he want sexy."

"I don't think that Janine's mom feels that way."

"Not good for children."

"They're going to be out of the house in a few years."

"They will be her children forever. If they divorce, their children will divorce, too. Happens like that. Mothers have to care for children first. Nobody else will do that. Not even fathers!"

My mother's unhappiness cemented the bond between us, as though the distance between her and Appa was inversely, causally related to the bond between us. She was my burden, my obligation, as I was hers.

I hear the door open and the bustling sounds of Ahma hanging up her purse and slipping off her shoes. She walks into the kitchen and sees me peering into the open refrigerator.

"You must have hungry," is the first thing she says. The second is, "Shut door. You waste electricity."

Ahma is wearing a sleeveless silk dress and a necklace with pearls the size of marbles. Her arm lacks the wattle that I remember she used to have when I was a teenager, that fatty roll that I've recently noticed slipping over the edges of my own sleeveless tees and tanks. I notice a white bag on the kitchen table.

"No food in refrigerator. I forgot to shopping. No, not forget, too busy."

In the bag is a Caesar salad and a BLT with avocado. There was a time when the idea of Ahma bringing home a BLT for dinner would have seemed absurd. When I was growing up, the house always smelled good at dinnertime. There was warm rice with every meal, some kind of meat or fish cooked in sesame oil, and half a dozen little side dishes of pickled or marinated vegetables and dried fish. I took it all for granted, just as I took for granted Appa's place at the head of the table, Ahma's traipsing back and forth from her seat to the kitchen, my family as it was then and, I assumed, always would be.

"I ate with client," she says. She sounds tired.

"Was it a date?"

She shrugs. "Maybe."

I take a bite of the sandwich. It is delicious, with just the right amount of mayo. The bacon and lettuce are still crisp.

"This is really good."

"Thanks to client."

"He paid? Then it was a date."

"Maybe." She looks troubled.

"I thought men were supposed to pay."

"Not if he's client. Better for me to pay for client. Client is better than date."

"He can be both, can't he?"

She shakes her head and clenches her face in annoyance. "Not professional."

Of course she's right. I hadn't really thought about it because it's never been an issue in my work life. Even with Louis out of my life, the prospects of meeting someone at work are dim. Harry is gay, Randolph Johnson is nearly eighty and married, and most of the supervisors at Restin are women. Except Mr. Park, but he's the age my father would have been if he were still alive.

"Anyway, I thought you were dating that doctor."

Ahma's face lights up, and she straightens her posture. "Have to play in field. Many fishes in sea."

"I thought he was such a catch."

"I not catch him. He try to catching me."

I take another bite of the sandwich, which is no longer as delicious as it was a minute ago. The toast is soggy from the tomato. There's not enough lettuce.

"Good night," she says, heading up the stairs.

"Good night," I say. The bacon in my mouth feels as dry and crumbly as sand.

That night I have a dream that I am making dinner. Ahma is sitting at my place at the dining room table. I am rushing back and forth, carrying plates of steaming spaghetti. The noodles are very long and drape over the edges of the plate, and huge meatballs sit in puddles of tomato sauce, like in a cartoon. I keep bringing more and more food to the table, hot cast-iron pots of kimchi stew, a tray of BLTs, a platter of barbecued short ribs. My face is dripping with sweat, and I am wearing a white apron and a chef's hat. Ahma is calm and cool and doesn't lift a finger to help me. In fact, she is painting her fingernails, seemingly oblivious to my tremendous expenditure of energy. She paints each nail a flaming orange, lifts it up, paints it and blows on it to dry, paints it some more. Her hair is big and fierce, like a supermodel from the nineties, but she doesn't look ridiculous. She doesn't really look like herself, either. She's Caucasian and about sixteen years old, but I know that it's her. There is a grunting sound in the background, and I think it's coming from me as I rush back and forth, back and forth. I don't know why I am in such a rush, since Ahma doesn't seem the least bit interested in the food. She just paints her nails and blows, and paints and admires. Then I realize that the grunting is not coming from me. I am cooking for my husband, who is sitting at the head of the table. In my dream, I suddenly stop and look at him, as though I just now realize I have a husband. He is furry, with giant paws for hands, like a giant grizzly bear, but something is wrong with his face. I can't figure out what it is, and then I realize that my husband has *no face*! Just fur but no eyes or nose. A furry faceless mug with a pit for a mouth that opens when he roars to express his disappointment at the horrible cook he married.

When I wake, I see that I am in my old room with the fading, peeling paint on the walls, the familiar white dresser with the fake gold trim, the books from my high school English class—*Madame Bovary, Pride and Prejudice, The Great Gatsby*. The house is quiet. I tiptoe downstairs. There is no grunting, faceless bear-ogre husband at the table. The kitchen is clean, the counters wiped down, and the dishes removed from the draining board.

∼

Of my three jobs, I like Restin best. It is my longest commute—usually a forty-minute drive because of the traffic—but I like the change of scenery. The town of Restin is in the hills, separated from its sexier and more glamorous sister, Restin Beach, by the interstate. Restin Beach is the ultimate Orange County city, with multimillion-dollar homes with ocean views, a Mercedes-Benz in every driveway, silicone in every breast, and Botox in every forehead. Restin, the town, is down to earth, less intimidating, and everyone drives a Ford pickup, a Honda, or a Prius. Most of the residents have lived there for decades, meaning that it's not a town filled with only wealthy C-level executives, venture capitalists, and plastic surgeons.

Thanks to some local legislation and zoning laws, development is limited, and the hills are unmarred by McMansions. There is a commercial district, which is just three short blocks, with a hardware store, a drug store with an old-fashioned ice cream counter, and a general store that sells jeans and Hanes T-shirts. It is a typical small town in an America that no longer exists, an anomaly in cutting-edge SoCal, where modernist houses built sixty years ago still look futuristic. The folks who live in Restin are wrinkled and friendly and let their hair go gray and their breasts sag, unlike their injection-filled neighbors across the interstate.

I would love to live in one of the cute cottage-like bungalows, but that can never be more than a dream. The homes, while not as expensive as those in Restin Beach, are still north of a million, thanks to the overheated real estate market in Southern California. In other words, far, far out of my free-lance bookkeeper's reach. I used to think, *Maybe, someday.* But I'm starting to realize that it's more likely to be *Never.* I'm plagued again by the nagging feeling that time is passing, but not in the way people talk about when they say, *Time flies!* Time for me doesn't fly so much as tiptoe past, as though trying not to draw attention to itself, like an early-departing guest at a bad party.

Tuesdays and Thursdays as I pass through town, I fantasize about living in one of the cute craftsman cottages with the brick porches and river rock chimneys. I might have a dog, a big friendly beast that wags its tail and lies loyally at my feet while I drink my morning cup of coffee and read the newspaper. I cook dinner in this house because it's a fantasy. There is a pot rack over the stove, and the whole house smells like freshly baked bread. There should be children in this fantasy and a husband who is sweet and sensitive and plays guitar in front of the fireplace. The kids are young, and there are two of them, a boy and a girl, or two girls, or two boys—it doesn't matter. What matters is that they are little and play nicely with each other, laughing happily while I bake bread and sing to the music that my soulful husband strums on his guitar . . .

But the harsh reality is that I don't know how to paint, can't carry a tune, and have never baked bread. I crunch numbers for a living, I'm allergic to dog hair, and I don't deserve to have any children. Anyway, Restin is out of my reach, like all my fantasies.

Today, I am in the back office of the library. I have to reconcile numbers from the last book sale. I'm angry at myself for having missed it. They were selling hardcovers for a dollar each. Mr. Park walks by as I am settling in at my desk. He is the director of library sciences.

"Good morning, Mrs. Markson," he says. "Long time, no see."

"Yeah, it's been busy," I say. I haven't told Mr. Park that Louis and I are divorcing. Why did I even bother changing my name when we got married?

I turn on my computer and wait for it to boot up.

"It's starting to be the busy season for this department now," he says.

I nod. He tells me that the library donated the funds from the book sale to an elementary school in Santa Ana where one of the librarian's daughters teaches fifth grade.

"It's not in the Restin school district?" I ask.

He shakes his head. "Does it have a fiscal impact?"

At first, I think he is asking whether it has a *physical* impact. Mr. Park's English is very good, but sometimes the rhythm of his speech is a little off and I have to process his words in the context of his sentence. My father had the same way of speaking. I have often thought about how much Mr. Park reminds me of my father. They even look similar, and not just because they are—were—both Korean men of about the same age. I wonder if Mr. Park knows anyone who could translate my father's notebook for me. Besides being Korean and the director of library sciences, he's also the head of the Multicultural Studies Collection. If anyone could help me, it would be him. He must know someone.

"No, no fiscal impact. I think it's great that the staff had a fundraiser for another school."

He smiles and nods. "Yes, good to share the wealth. Sarah's daughter told her that the students in her class have to share textbooks because there are too many students and not enough money for books. Outrageous! Meanwhile, Restin schools have a surplus every year."

Mr. Park often shakes his head that a country as rich as ours doesn't have better social services, cheaper health care, or more accessible public transportation. He has a "Pro-Choice" bumper sticker on his Prius, and his desk is littered with donation receipts from various causes and thank-you notes from organizations like Planned Parenthood, Amnesty International, Doctors without Borders, and HANA, an environmental group in Hawaii, where he grew up. He's so different from my parents' friends, who seem more interested in their golf handicap and designer handbags than climate change or income inequality. Even living in idyllic, time-warped Restin, he manages to stay informed. He will often make comments about current events or cultural references that just make me blink with confusion. Maybe he reads *People* magazine on the can. But that can't be it. I know, because *I* read *People* on the can, and that hasn't improved my ability to make conversation or given me any interesting insights on global warming.

"Where do you live?"

I'm a little taken aback by his question. Mr. Park rarely asks me anything about myself. He is friendly enough, but our conversations have never been about anything personal—except, of course, politics, if you believe that all politics are personal.

"Um . . . in Green Hills," I say. He nods his head, and I can guess what he is thinking. Country club, politically apathetic, luxury-car driving, designer-label obsessed. Typical Orange County Korean American.

"Your parents golf?"

I nod. "My mother does. My father's dead."

Mr. Park looks shocked and a little embarrassed, which is precisely the reaction I want. I didn't need to tell him that my father is dead, of course. But it bothers me that he thinks he knows what I'm about.

"I'm sorry."

I shrug. "Yeah, so am I."

I turn back to my computer. Mr. Park stands quietly for a moment and then walks away.

CHAPTER FIVE

Ahma is not home when I get back Wednesday evening, but she left a foil-wrapped container on the counter. I open it. *Bindaeduk.* Korean mung bean pancakes with peppers and pork. She even prepared a small bowl of vinegar and soy dipping sauce. There is no note.

I microwave my dinner and then plop down on the couch, in front of the TV. The bindaeduk is delicious, even though I microwaved it instead of frying it in the cast-iron pan. With my fingers, I pull apart a piece of the bindaeduk and dip it into the sauce. I taste the fluffy meal, soaked in the spicy salty-sweet sauce, and then the other goodies inside—thin slices of tender pork, slivers of sautéed chili, red bell peppers, and buttery leek. Eating this reminds me of my father. We used to sit on the couch together and eat bindaeduk, with a beer for him and a glass of milk for me. If either of us had suggested that Ahma come and join us, she probably would have protested that she had too much to do, that dinner would never get done, and that beer made her dizzy. But the suggestion was never made, so Ahma never had an opportunity to so adamantly refuse.

The sound of the door opening startles me. It takes me a moment to realize that it is only Ahma and that I have fallen asleep on the couch with my empty plate on the coffee table, the bowl of sauce giving the room a slightly fermented smell. I quickly pick up my plate and the bowl and take them to the kitchen, giving each a brief rinse before sticking them both into the dishwasher. Ahma doesn't call my name the way she usually does, and my heart quickens for an instant. Something doesn't feel right. Maybe it's not Ahma but an intruder? Would a burglar use the front door? I recall reading somewhere that most burglars use an open window or an unlocked door—the path of least resistance.

"Ahma?" I call softly, as though my whisper were something that burglars couldn't hear but mothers could.

The shuffling in the entryway stops. I peer around the corner of the kitchen wall and see Ahma's figure in the darkness. I am relieved that she is alone.

"What are you doing? You scared me!"

She doesn't laugh. "Did you eat dinner?"

"Yes, did you?" I hope I wasn't supposed to leave a pancake for her.

"Yes."

She is still standing in the entryway, as though she is afraid to come into the house, and she is avoiding looking at me directly, as though she is afraid of me. I take a few steps toward her, and she turns around and spends too much time taking off her shoes. "Where did you go?"

Ahma finally stands. Her hair is messy, and her lipstick and mascara are smeared. The undefined dread that has been coursing through my blood solidifies in the pit of my stomach like poured cement.

"What happened?"

"Not your business."

"Did you get fired?"

She frowns and shakes her head.

"What happened?"

"Crazy man. So crazy!"

"A crazy man attacked you?"

Ahma's face is a mask that would crack with the right question, but so far, I am not asking it.

"Some crazy man on the street attacked you? Did he take your purse?"

She shakes her head.

"Was it someone you know?"

She nods her head, and her eyes fill with tears. "Why you still awake. You should sleeping!"

I know what she really means. *If you didn't live here with me, you wouldn't know of my humiliation.*

"Who was it?"

She starts to walk upstairs.

"Was it a client? Somebody you work with?"

"No worry for you. Mind your business."

"Was it Stephen?"

My mother's head is held high as she nods once. I follow her up the stairs.

I sit on the bed while she showers and brushes her teeth. I wait until she is in her nightgown and tucked underneath the covers. I wait while she turns off the lamp next to her bed so that I can't see her shame. She talks to me, in Korean, in a voice that droops with sadness and pain. I don't understand some of the words, because they are words that I never had to learn, grown-up words, but I am able to guess their meaning from the context.

She and Stephen had met for dinner again. They went to a nice restaurant, and she let him pay. He surprised her with a present, a gold charm bracelet with one charm—a squash racket. He told her that he would buy her a surfboard charm next, after he taught her to surf. When he suggested that they go back to his house, she agreed, even though it was late and she was tired. He made her a drink, even though she doesn't drink. She accepted the invitation because she was being polite, and she accepted the drink because she knew that he didn't want to drink alone. They sat on the couch and he put on music, and Stephen started to kiss her. My mother was alarmed and uncomfortable; he smelled funny up close—"like wet laundry that forgot to put in dryer"—but she didn't want to hurt his feelings since he had been so nice to her, had taken her to dinner, and had bought her a present. Because she felt so neutral about him, she underestimated how excited he was getting. She thought that she would tell him that she had to go soon, after he had a few more kisses, "maybe five or six kisses to make fair," but she couldn't find the right break in between the kisses because he didn't seem to need air, and he went over his maximum-kiss limit.

"Then, fast as magician, he naked," she says, switching to English.

I am not sure that I want to hear what happened next.

"He look so funny. I laughing."

"You laughed?"

Ahma nods. "He look like little boy. Only more hair."

I know that laugh, the insensitive cackle of a mother at her awkward daughter. I have heard it enough times to know how cruel it sounds to vulnerable ears. I can't help feeling a little bit sorry for Stephen.

"So hairy! Like bear. Hair everywhere."

I do not want this visual of naked Stephen.

"Not like your father. Your father's chest smooth as baby bottom."

I *really* do not want this visual of my father.

"Stephen chest hairy. Bottom too! Like gorilla."

"Ahma!"

She laughs. Despite myself, I laugh, too.

"He mad but even more excited. He talking nasty words. Try to kiss me again with his trash mouth."

"Nasty words?"

"Ooh baby. Like bad movie on cable. But I told him I have to go home. He got mad and push me. He yell, too. He tell me to leave his house and never come again."

"What did you do?"

"I tell him I want to leave very much. He never want to see me again. Me too, I say. Then you know what?"

"What?"

"He say he want present back."

41

She shakes her head. "Can you believe? He thought my worth equals only a cheap bracelet with one charm."

Ahma doesn't seem so upset after she finishes telling me her story. In fact, she almost seems to be in good spirits. There is no need for me to stay with her and comfort her, since somehow I am now the one in need of comforting and she has quickly fallen asleep. While she quietly snores next to me, I lie on top of the covers, anxious about my mother's entry into the modern world of dating. She is so naive sometimes! She dresses in sexy clothing that shows off her figure, accepts expensive presents, and agrees to nightcaps at the homes of men she barely knows. I know that a woman should be able to do all those things, and it shouldn't mean she has to put out. I know that no means no, that paying for dinner does not mean paying for sex. But I also know that sometimes, things are not the way I want them to be and that the world is full of men who take without asking, who assume certain things about a woman based upon what she looks like and how she dresses. I know that until there is a baseline of mutual understanding, it is important to be cautious, look both ways, and always wear your seat belt. But Ahma, not Ahma! She accepts dates from strangers at the gym, wears clothing that is a size too small and a generation too young, and laughs at naked men. She is completely ignorant about the rules of social conduct.

But no, something is not right in that characterization.

Ahma was the one who lectured me before I went off to college about the dangers of drinking and boys and sex, with and without condoms. She was the one who made me change my clothes when I showed up at the breakfast table wearing a skirt that was too short or a sweater that was too tight. When I protested, "I am not a slut! It doesn't matter what other people think because of the way I dress—that's their problem, not mine!" she calmly provided an explanation of the social meaning of clothes that would have made Roland Barthes proud. And the fact was, she was right, and I knew it, even though I didn't want to accept it and wanted to rebel against it.

I am reminded of a picture I saw at a museum once, a black-and-white drawing of two black faces, or was it a white goblet? The more I stared at the picture, the harder it was to tell what it was, and the images seemed to flicker from one to the other. A figure-ground illusion. This is an entirely different situation from what I had initially thought.

Ahma is not a rebel, but she is practical. She made her calculation. Tight jeans and a sassy attitude garner male attention. The occasional unwanted advance is a hazard but one that she can handle. She escaped Stephen's house fully clothed and has already recovered. Stephen, on the other hand, may never be the same.

My eyes have adjusted to the darkness, and I can see Ahma's sleeping face. Her mouth is slightly open and she is snoring. Her eyeballs roll underneath her closed eyelids. I hope she is having a pleasant dream.

I gently lift myself off the bed, so as not to wake her, and make my way downstairs. The moonlight shines through the open curtains, and I see Ahma's purse at the bottom of the stairs, gaping open like an invitation. The image shifts again. The white box sits like an egg in its nest. I lift the lid and take out the gold bracelet. The charm dangles limply, a racket looking for a match.

~

The next morning, Ahma acts as though nothing has happened. I don't mention the charm bracelet, and neither does she. She asks me if I want pancakes, and I shake my head.

"You not late?" she asks as she pours the mix into a bowl.

"No."

"Good. Not good to be always late." She adds water and stirs.

"I said I didn't want pancakes."

"Pancake good for you. Have to eat breakfast."

"I know, but it doesn't have to be pancakes."

She slices a banana and puts it into the pancake batter.

"Why do you always pretend that you are doing something for me when it's actually for you?"

She ladles the batter onto the hot frying pan and gets a plate out of the cabinet.

"I hate bananas," I add. "And I am sick of pancakes. You love banana pancakes. Why don't you just make the pancakes for yourself and cut the pretense that you are doing something nice for me?"

"Selfish girl," she mutters. She flips the pancake.

"I'm not the selfish one! I'm just asking you why you have to pretend like that. It's dishonest. It's a lie."

She lifts the pancake off the pan and onto the plate, and then hands it to me.

"Ha! *You* the liar."

She looks at me hard, and in that moment, I realize that she knows the truth about me and Louis, that the separation isn't temporary and we are getting a divorce. I take the plate. Ahma picks up her purse, slips on her shoes, and, without eating a single bite of breakfast, is out the door.

I sit down at the kitchen table and pick up the pancake with my fingers. The brown edges look deliciously crisp, the center pale and soft, and despite my convictions, I can't resist taking a bite. It's fluffy inside, and although I usually don't like bananas, these cooked slices are creamy and sweet. Only Ahma could make a pancake this good from a mix. I make more pancakes using the rest of the mix, but somehow they don't taste as good. I devour the stack anyway and polish off a tall glass of milk. I long for a cup of strong coffee, but Ahma doesn't have anything but a jar of old instant in the cabinets. I can pick up a latte at the drive-through Starbucks when I get off the freeway.

I finish my morning ritual—brush teeth, comb hair, apply lipstick, slip into shoes. I run downstairs, open the front door, stop, and then turn and run back upstairs. I grab the yellow envelope from the back of my closet, where I have hidden it at the bottom of a box of sweaters. I pull it out and cradle it to my chest. I need some answers, although to what questions, I don't know.

~

Mr. Park is carrying a large box into the room at about the same time that I am settling in at my desk with an overpriced latte.

"Doughnuts?" I ask.

"Cake!" He is smiling, and his whole face shines like a light bulb.

"Isn't it too early for cake?" groans Bertha. She is perpetually on a diet and resents all temptations but resists none.

"Never too early for cake!"

"What are we celebrating?"

"My son's birthday! He doesn't like cake, but I do!"

Everyone gathers around Mr. Park. Bertha is first in line, holding out her paper plate like a child at a birthday party. Mr. Park often talks about his son, Victor, who by all accounts is handsome, charming, smart, and committed to social justice. He was an EMT before he went to law school, and now he is going to help build schools for children someplace in Central America. He sounds too good to be true, and I would dismiss Mr. Park's claims as the delusional tales of a proud parent if the other women didn't corroborate them.

"Handsome as a movie star," Elaine says. "You'd never believe he was Sam's son!"

"It's true," Bertha whispers to me through a mouthful of frosting. "He is *all that*. Too bad he's only twenty-six." I nod sympathetically. Bertha has been much nicer since she found out that Louis and I split up. Even more disturbingly, she has started to *bond* with me over single-gal issues like the lack of good men, the perils of online dating, and the importance of losing ten pesky pounds. I usually nod and hope that she will not one day ask me to join her for a girls' night out on the town. I already have Janine for that sort of humiliation.

45

Later that day, I find Mr. Park in the courtyard, partially hidden by the container bamboo. He is standing with legs apart, in a classic warrior pose. My father stretched every morning, too, but that didn't keep him alive.

"Mr. Park?" Although the other women in the library call him Sam, it is impossible for me.

He lowers his arms to his sides and turns to me with the grace of a ballet dancer.

"Mrs. Markson," he says. Mr. Park has always referred to me formally as Mrs. Markson, which is odd, because I expect someone as politically aware as he is to use *Ms*. It's even odder because he's on a first-name basis with everyone else in the library. It might be because I'm only a glorified temp at Restin, but it might also be that, in the same way I can't see him as "Sam," he can't see me as "Ms. Markson" or even just "Alice."

"I'm sorry if I startled you. Is this an okay time to talk? I know you're on your lunch hour."

"Fine, fine. I was just finishing up anyway." He waits patiently, his round face a question mark.

"I was wondering whether you knew any translators that might not charge very much."

"Depends on which language."

"Korean," I say.

"That's a little tougher," he says. "Spanish, French, Italian, Japanese . . . but Korean, not so many. They will charge you an arm and a leg."

I already know this from my online research. It will cost at least $2,000, probably more, because of the number of characters. All the translation agencies charge per word.

"Is there someone you know who could do it? Someone who might charge me less than a professional?"

He smiles. "Funny thing is, everyone I know who is a native speaker could not translate it for you very well. Korean is not a hard language to learn, but it is not so popular, either."

"I feel like I should have learned it myself. I mean, I can speak it and understand it, but I just can't read Korean." I feel defensive, remembering times in the past when my parents and their friends chided me, "You have a Korean face. You should be able to speak Korean." But how could I learn if there was no one to teach me?

As though he can read my mind, he says, "Not so easy to find an instructor. I tried to find one for my son when he was younger, with no luck. And I am not patient enough." He smiles and adds, "My son is fluent in Spanish, though."

It is not the first time I have been struck by Mr. Park's empathy. He knows that I feel embarrassed to be in this position.

"Is it an official text? If you don't mind me asking?"

"No . . . it's just a notebook that my father left behind. I don't think it's anything terribly important. Probably something to do with his work."

"I might be able to help if you just want to know what it says. My skills may not be good enough if it is a business document, but if it is just for you and you don't need an official translation, I can do it as a favor."

"Oh no," I say. "I wouldn't want to trouble you. I mean, that would be very nice. I really appreciate it, but . . ." *But what?* I don't have other options. *Should I?* It's tempting, but I'm not sure that I want Mr. Park to know what is in my father's notebook.

"I don't think it will be much work for me. But if it contains legal or technical words, I might have to look them up. I think I have a Korean-English business dictionary somewhere in my office."

Maybe I should let him. It *could* just be a journal of my father's dental practice. But in my heart, I know it's something personal, and to let Mr. Park read it would be an invasion of my father's privacy. But does his privacy matter now to anyone but me and Ahma? And if she never knows, what difference could it make?

"It's rather long. About fifty pages," I say, in the interest of full disclosure.

"Perhaps you don't trust my ability?" He is smiling, but I wonder whether I have offended him with my reluctance.

"No, I don't mean it like that," I say quickly. "I just don't want to trouble you."

"No trouble. No rush, right?"

"Right. I mean, it's probably nothing important. But just in case it contains helpful information about his dental practice. One of the other dentists took it over, I think . . ." I am talking too much, trying to justify my unseemly desire to poke my nose into my father's business.

"Understandable. You are curious. It could be important."

"It's probably not, but I should find out."

He nods. "Yes. Lots of mysteries when somebody dies." Suddenly, he looks very sad. I remember hearing that Mr. Park's wife died earlier this year, sometime after the holidays, before I started working here.

"I really appreciate it. I'm happy . . . to compensate . . ."

His expression changes, and I know that I have made a grave mistake in offering. I quickly pivot: "By balancing your personal checkbook or organizing your home office files, or even taking out your trash on a weekly basis."

He laughs again. All is forgiven.

"Your mother doesn't read Korean?"

I look at the bamboo waving behind Mr. Park's head. I remember when they installed these pots in the courtyard. It was his idea to provide shade from the sun, so people could enjoy their breaks and lunches outside. But most of the time, the courtyard is still empty.

"I don't want to trouble her. She's still so upset, and she has so much to deal with . . ."

He nods. "Of course. If you have it today, please drop it by my office. I can take it when I leave tonight."

"Thank you, Mr. Park. I really appreciate it. Thank you very much."

LOVE AND LONELINESS

CHAPTER SIX

I am sitting at my desk, reading the latest newsletter from HANA, a nonprofit working to preserve Hawaii's environment and cultural heritage. I see that the organization is looking for an "archivist-specialist" to organize and collect materials for its new library. I imagine applying for that position, wonder what it would be like to return to Hawaii. The organization does good work, and I wish I could do more than write a check every few months. Although I am contributing to society at my current job, I often have the feeling that I could do more to help make the world a better place. But my life is here now, and it would be impossible to return home.

There is a soft knock at the door. I drop the newsletter in the recycling box that I have by my desk and call, "Come in."

It is Alice Markson, and she apologizes for the interruption. She reminds me of our previous conversation and hands me an envelope. The envelope is thick, but it is not the work that it contains that makes me feel uneasy. It is the way she looks, apologetic and flustered. She is a banana, a girl who is completely American except for her dark hair and her facial features. Even her physical build is Western, her bones large and strong from drinking gallons of cow's milk, her muscles developed from an abundance of meat and eggs and athletics. There is nothing Korean about her name, Alice Markson, which makes me think of gingham dresses, raccoon-tail caps, and rifles. Yet, when she hands me the envelope, she is distinctly Asian in the way she offers thanks, the instinctive bow of her spine, the nod of her head, the way she backs out of my small office, thanking, thanking, thanking me for a task that I have not yet undertaken. I hold the envelope in my hands, feeling the weight of the words within. Already, I fear that I have promised too much—not because the task exceeds my skills but because it might compromise me somehow.

~

Last night, Victor and I had a quiet dinner, just the two of us. I didn't get him a gift, even though it was his birthday. Birthdays and holidays make us both uncomfortably aware of who is absent. His mother used to take care of the details when she was here living with us. At least during the time when she still cared.

Expressive words, terms of endearment, occasions that require presents—all make me shift with discomfort. For me, the display creates distance rather than intimacy. What should I say: "I'm proud of you, son"? Those words, coming from me, would sound false. I imagine they would make Victor feel uncomfortable as well, or am I wrong? Does he expect celebrations, rites of passage? Should I have bought him a present? I brought a cake into the office because my coworkers like sweets and because they are not so close to me. I can celebrate with them because the celebration creates the meaning. But with Victor? Everything means so much. I don't really know what he expects. He seems to have grown up on his own, under my nose, while I was distracted by his mother.

Tonight, Victor is out with friends, having a proper birthday celebration. I imagine there will be music and laughter. I hope there will be lots of laughter. I fix myself a cup of *genmai cha*, tea that will both calm and revive me. I sit at the dining room table and think about making dinner, but I am not hungry. I remember the notebook that yesterday I promised to translate for Alice. I retrieve it from my backpack and undo the metal clasp, slide my index finger underneath the flap of the envelope, and pull out the notebook. After a few words, I realize that this is not a business journal. This is a man's private thoughts. I know I shouldn't continue, but his voice compels me. There is something familiar about it. Is it possible that I knew Alice's father? There aren't many Koreans of our generation in this part of Orange County. We were the pioneers. The ones who had to explain when we were asked, "Where are you from?" that Korea wasn't China, Japan, or Vietnam, even though Americans had fought a war there, too. Maybe I knew him. I continue reading despite my misgivings, looking for clues.

~

January 8, 2010

I had a dream last night that was so real that I am still uncertain if I was asleep. I was standing on the bank of a rushing river. On the other side was a figure, calling to me. The sound of the water was too loud for me to understand anything but the name she used, a name that only she and I knew. I stood on tiptoe, straining to see more clearly. Was it really her? She smiled and waved, beckoning me to join her. I wanted to swim out to her, but when I touched my toe to the water, I was too afraid of the cold, rushing current. I looked over at her, and her smile was sad. Then her features started to blur and melt away.

"I'm sorry," I said, and she disappeared.
Why now, after so many years?

~

January 16, 2010

I write these words hoping that they will help me understand. It's been so many years. Why does her image haunt me? Again, last night, I dreamed of the ghostly presence calling to me from the other side of the river. But why, and what does it mean? I am a married man, mostly happy, with a lovely daughter and a thriving dental practice. Other men would envy me and want nothing more, but my heart still yearns, even after fifty years. How would my life have turned out differently if I had followed my desires rather than run from my fears? I will always wonder. And so, I write to try to make sense of that time.

I remember the day clearly. I was playing soccer in the courtyard with my friends. It was a hot day, even though it was already September and the leaves had started to fall. Still, we played like fools, running in the dirt, kicking each other in the shins more often than we managed to kick the ball. I saw my father standing in the courtyard. Next to him stood a tall white man wearing a pressed white shirt, gray slacks, and black-rimmed spectacles. He was holding the hand of a girl of about fifteen, my age. She had curly shoulder-length hair the color of wheat. A tortoiseshell barrette held it out of her face.

I don't remember exactly what happened next, although my mother probably called me into the house. I remember sitting on the floor in my parents' house and worrying that my mother would scold me for sitting on the silk pillow with my sweaty bottom. Across from me sat the girl, wearing a navy-blue jumper with a white shirt. My own shirt was soiled because I had worn it for several days. She smiled at me. I was in love even before I knew her name.

Her father was a missionary educator, meaning that he taught English but he also taught us about the Lord Jesus Christ. It was the first time I heard it pronounced that way. My mother always talked about Yesoo Christo, and it took me a while before I realized that Mr. Smith and my mother were talking about the same son of God. My mother was a newly converted Christian, and my father's English was pretty good compared to others in the neighborhood, which I guess is why they chose to dine with us every now and then, usually on Sunday evenings. Before the girl was born, her parents had lived in Korea when it was still under Japanese rule. They spoke Korean surprisingly well for Americans. Even the girl could converse a little in the language, although with great difficulty. I could understand some English, as it was taught to us in school. We pieced together our conversations, weaving together words in Korean, words in English, until we thought we understood each other. I learned that her name was Shirley, but I can't remember whether she herself told me or whether it was her father, or maybe my father, or maybe I just heard her father call her by this name. It is a name that I cannot say, even to this day.

"Shoodee."

She looked annoyed. She held my chin between her fingers. "Say it right. Shurly. Shurrrly. Try."

"Shooodeeee. Shoooddeeee." I knew the sounds were wrong as they came out of my mouth but couldn't get them right.

She smiled at my efforts. Her smile lit me up, like a match tossed into a pile of straw.

~

January 20, 2010

The war that aimed to unite the North and South succeeded only in hardening the division and upended the world for my parents, both of whom had relatives in the North. My mother had a sister, an aunt and uncle, and three cousins. My father had an older brother. In the years that followed the end of the war, on top of everything else, they had to reconcile themselves to the idea that they would never see these relatives again. There were stories, too. They heard that in the North, people were routinely tortured and killed. They heard that people were starving, and they had no books, no music. My parents were haunted by these stories. Even as others in our neighborhood gradually recovered from the war, my parents never did.

Growing up, we never had enough food. I remember waiting in line to receive handouts from the American missionaries. We viewed them as our saviors, and we were grateful for what they gave us—the corned beef hash that we ate out of tin cans with our fingers and the stale bread that we gnawed at like hungry mice.

Our house had no plumbing, so we used a hole in the ground behind the house. My parents clung to their education and their cultivation, since they didn't have much else. My younger sister was sick with a coughing disease—it was likely tuberculosis, but there was no name for it that I can remember—and my mother was preoccupied. She must have been relieved when I was out of the house.

My parents did not seem to mind that I spent the days with Shirley. They understood that she was different because she was the daughter of American missionaries. She was blessed by God.

Shirley picked up Korean words easily for a foreigner, although she often stressed the wrong parts of words or emphasized the wrong syllable, so that it was difficult to understand her at first. Communicating with her took patience and effort. She was desperate for friends, but the other kids were intimidated by her wide gestures and her rough Korean, and they were unable to communicate with her in English. When she saw me on the street after our first meeting, she smiled and held out her hand. In it, she was holding an orange. I stared at her and looked nervously around, hoping that my schoolmates hadn't seen. They would swarm around her and take all of it. I motioned for her to follow me. I led her to the back of a rundown shop where an angry dog was tied to a tree. It growled at us menacingly, but the *ribs poking through its skin reassured us that it would not have the energy to break free. We crouched on the ground, and she peeled the orange. She pulled it apart and offered me half. Half! Such generosity. I would have been satisfied with one small section. I can still smell the orange and taste the juice. I was so grateful to her.*

After we ate the orange, we went for a walk. We passed another dog, this time a big shaggy one, lying underneath a large tree.

"Why isn't it tied?" Shirley wondered, nervous after our encounter with the first dog.

"I know that dog. He belongs to my neighbor. He won't run off anywhere. He is very old. My mother says that he will die soon."

We watched the ailing dog.

"His legs are bleeding. Did he cut himself?"

"No, my mother says his legs are too stiff to carry him. He gnaws on them because he thinks it will relieve the pain inside. Instead, it just makes it worse."

Shirley shuddered. "Poor dog. Somebody should put him out of his misery."

Until that moment, it had never occurred to me that an animal would be better off dead than alive and suffering.

~

January 27, 2010

Today, I returned from work with a feeling of great sadness. My wife had prepared a wonderful supper of fried tofu and mackerel. The house was clean. She was smiling brightly. Yet, her very cheeriness depressed me. The bright smile on her face deepened the lines around her eyes and showed off the yellowness of her teeth. The adoration that shone in her eyes blinded her to the disinterest in my own. She waited like an obedient dog while I washed my hands and changed my clothes. She enjoyed the meal with each bite that I took, while her own plate remained untouched.

The meal was delicious. The mackerel was expertly poached in chige so that it was tender and moist inside and spicy and salty outside. The tofu was fried to perfection, the edges crisp, the inside silky as cream. But the deliciousness of the meal only made me more irritated. Why does she spend all day cooking meals for me? So that we can chew in silence? She has nothing to offer me. No stories to tell, no wisdom to share. Only perfectly cooked fish and fried tofu. While I toil away to make a living, she shops and cleans and cooks all day, every day. It is hardly surprising, then, that she has nothing interesting to say to me when I come home. Our life together has become predictable and so dull that sometimes I want to flee. But she suspects nothing. After nearly four decades together, she is unable to decipher the clues I offer her about my unhappiness. I can only think of two explanations for her surprising lack of perceptiveness. Either she is stupid or she is fooling herself. Both explanations are unflattering to her and reinforce my belief that I made an awful mistake in selecting her to be my wife. My lifelong partner is stupid? My lifelong partner is self-deceptive? There is a third option, but it is unlikely. Perhaps she senses my unhappiness but just doesn't care. I reject this third option, because if she truly did not care, then she would not go through the effort of fixing a delicious meal for me every night. Even tonight, she started to eat only after offering me seconds. After all these years in this country, I have never understood how my wife has remained so traditional. Even in modern Korea, the women are not so subservient to their husbands. It is as if we are living in a time capsule, only I manage to escape for hours each workday and for most of the blissful night. For it is at night when Shirley has started to visit me.

Last night she came wearing a housedress with coverall straps. She smiled as she kissed me on the mouth. She removed her dress, slipping the denim straps off her shoulders as though they were made of silk and lace. Her body glowed with youth and vitality. Her hair glimmered like gold. I, too, was as youthful as she. We floated toward each other and consummated our desire for each other in midair. In the nonsensical manner of dreams, we were floating above a busy city street, and I could hear the sound of cars honking and people cheering below us. It started to rain. The water felt cool and cleansing. When I awoke, I was drenched in sweat. I had ejaculated in my pajama bottoms as though I were a teenager. My poor wife remained sleeping next to me, suspecting nothing.

~

January 30, 2010

Shirley comes to visit me every night. Sometimes she awakens me with a whisper. She calls the name that she gave me. It is an American name, simple and generic. John. She never wanted to use my Korean name, Il Joo, and I never made her. She remade me in her own eyes, and I happily succumbed. My new name was nondescript, a blank canvas upon which I allowed her to rewrite my identity.

I was exotic to her, foreign, even though she was the one who was the foreigner. She would stay only for a few months. She was surrounded by those who looked like me, but I was the one who was different. I was the one who had to explain myself to her. Why did I take off my shoes inside the house? Why did I eat dried cuttlefish? Why did I not smile, even when I felt happy? We both knew that I was the one who was irregular while she was the norm, the point of reference. I had never seen anyone like her in the flesh, yet she was familiar. Her blue eyes and her big teeth and her wavy hair. Her smile was open and welcoming, hiding nothing. She was the image I had seen in magazines, in the movies. Even her name was familiar. Shoo-dee. Shirley. Like the movie star with the bouncy ringlets and the tapping feet. Like the sweet drink with the fancy candied cherry and the fizzy bubbles that sting the nose. Her image haunts me in my dreams. Wake up, John.

I sit up, listening to the sound of her voice, which I can still hear clearly, even though my eyes are open. I turn to my wife, who doesn't hear anything.

She sleeps with a clenched face, as though she knows that she is losing me to a memory. I want to tell her not to fear, for there is nothing to lose. It is too late. I am already lost.

~

February 3, 2010

Why do I remember all of this so clearly, as though it happened just yesterday? She was the love of my life. When she kissed me, I thought I had died and gone to heaven. The pleasure was so sweet that I knew I would burn in hell. Her parents visited occasionally, bringing vegetables and canned goods. Sometimes they stayed for dinner, and afterward, the grown-ups would go for a walk. Sometimes Shirley and I would join them, but as we became more familiar with each other, we declined their invitations. I wonder now whether this was craftiness on her part. Did she intend to seduce me from the start? Or did the idea unfold before her slowly as we spent more time together? Did I become more appealing to her as she got to know me?

"Come here," she said. "No, over here."

She leaned her head toward me so suddenly that I instinctively moved back.

"Stay still."

I stared at her. Her eyes closed, and she pursed her lips and pressed them to mine. She frowned slightly and pulled away. She opened her mouth but not her eyes. My mouth had fallen open in surprise. She leaned toward me again. This time, I could not move. I felt her tongue against mine. I thought I would die.

One thing is certain. I had no say in the matter. I would do whatever she asked. I would lie, steal, beg, borrow. I would betray my parents and my friends and myself.

One thing I did not know then, but I know is true now, is that I had also betrayed my future. My future wife, my future family. My future self. The memory of her taints my existence even now. How can I say I love my wife when I know that I once loved someone much more? I can never love anyone the way I loved Shirley. Would I still love her if I saw her again?

She is probably fat now. She is probably wide in the hips and thick in the thighs and middle. She probably has fatty arms that jiggle when she waves them. She probably wears glasses. She is probably wrinkly and wobbly. Yet I would still love her, I would still want her. I know it as certainly as I know anything.

Do I regret anything? Would I have resisted, knowing that she would destroy all possibility for any real happiness with anyone else? That my life afterward would be only black and white, shadows and shapes without definition?

~

February 6, 2010

The memories are now more intense. This is what it means to grow old. I am more alive in my head than in my body. But back then, I lived through my body. Where was my head? Where was my head when I agreed to meet Shirley in the woods behind the school? My feet were present as they marched me to our meeting spot. My heart was present as it pounded in my chest. Perhaps that was all there was to me back then.

The air was crisp and cold. The sky was clear. I smelled smoke from a neighbor's fire, heard the cries of my friends as they played at the schoolyard. I walked past them, ignoring their greetings, their questions. I turned the corner, toward the woods. The leaves had turned on most of the maple trees. Pine cones littered the ground, and I kicked them as I hurried past. I saw Shirley up ahead. She was wearing her blue jumper with a white shirt. She raised one hand and waved. I ran to her.

"Why did you ask me to meet you?" I wanted to pull her into my arms but was afraid.

She smiled at me in her lopsided manner. She reached out to me and did what I wanted to do to her. She pulled me so close against her that I could feel her heart race.

"Wait," she whispered.

I could do nothing else. She took one of my hands and placed it underneath her shirt. She kissed me on the mouth, her tongue prying apart my lips. I reached my other hand underneath her jumper.

It began like that. Slowly, at first. Then, one day, we were not able to stop.

~

I look at the characters carefully scripted onto the page. I have no business reading this. Everyone is entitled to their secrets. These are a man's most private thoughts, his personal memories. I am convinced Alice's father did not intend for anyone else to read this. He probably did not expect to die. He would die again if he knew his notebook was in his daughter's possession, that it is now in the hands of a complete stranger.

I will explain to Alice Markson that this notebook is not meant for me to read. It is not something that she herself should read. She will understand when I tell her that I do not feel comfortable, that I did not know what I was agreeing to do. Surely she herself did not know what she was handing over to me. Even if she suspected that it was a personal diary, she could not have guessed what it would reveal.

Or maybe I will tell her that I am busier than I thought, that I have no time to translate this for her. I do not want her to know that I have read even this much of it, that I have accessed her father's most private memories. She would feel deceived and wonder why I did not stop immediately. She would be right to wonder. I should not have read even as much as I have.

I close the notebook and slide it back into the yellow envelope, pressing down on the metal clasp to secure it. I resolve that I will return it to Alice on Tuesday.

CHAPTER SEVEN

I am trying to fall asleep, but my mind is racing with worries about giving my father's notebook to Mr. Park yesterday. What if Mr. Park knew my father? The Korean community in this area is still relatively small and tightly knit, at least for my parents' generation. But I can't spend the rest of my life wondering what it says, and I'll probably never be able to afford to pay a real translator.

But my father's notebook isn't the only thing that is keeping me awake. Earlier tonight, I met Janine for dinner at El Toreador. She was unusually contemplative. The musician she picked up last weekend hadn't called, and she saw an old boyfriend—or lover, anyway—at the post office.

"He was standing in this long line because he had to mail a package"—she paused for dramatic effect—"for his wife."

She tried to give me a wry look, but the tears in her eyes undermined the effort. "She was at home nursing their newborn."

Janine took a long sip of her margarita. She reached out and grabbed a chip but didn't eat it. "It wasn't even that long ago that we stopped seeing each other." She crumbled the chip between her fingers. "What am I talking about? It wasn't that long ago that *he* stopped calling *me*."

This time, I took a long sip of my margarita.

"It was less than a year ago. So what does that mean? That he met his wife the day after he decided that I wasn't right for him, and then they got married right away and poof! A year later, instant family. It takes nine months to make a baby, right? At least, that's what I *heard*. Not that I would have any experience with that. This is a guy who was so incredibly selfish that he never took me out to dinner, never picked me up to go anywhere. I always had to meet him, at his apartment, like some call girl who wasn't even worth paying. And now, here he is at the post office, waiting in a long line for his *wife*, who's at home with his new baby! And he looked happy, too. Not like she tricked him and got pregnant. He was so proud! He even showed me this horrid picture of the baby all covered in blood with the umbilical cord still attached."

"Yuck. Why do people always show pictures of newborns? They are not cute."

Janine shook her head. "Why is it always someone else? What is it about me that makes them run so fast? I used to kid myself that it was because I was too hot for them to handle, too independent and wild. But now I think that maybe they just think I'm not good enough. I'm good enough to bang, and that's it. And I won't even be good enough for that in a few years . . ."

Janine started to cry then, her mouth crumpling like a bird's broken wing. I've seen this look over the years, and it always frightens me because it's so different from the happy face that she usually puts on. Tonight, though, mascara blackened her eyes like bruises, and the tears made streaks through her makeup. Her cheeks were red from tequila and crying. I had a scary vision of us, twenty years from now, bitter and angry at the world for what it had failed to deliver.

"Listen," I said, handing her a cocktail napkin. "Stop it. Stop feeling sorry for yourself. You told me about that guy. You said he was awful in bed, that all he cared about was getting off, and then he was out the door. So why would you want to be married to someone like that? And as for meeting someone perfect the day after he stopped calling you, what makes you think that he wasn't two-timing both of you? Maybe his girlfriend found out? Maybe *you* were the other woman, and he never told you that he was married?"

"He was at the post office, mailing a package for her . . ."

"So what? That's what people do when they're married to each other. They do errands for each other. That doesn't mean that he met some woman and *changed*. And even if he did, why do you care? You have a say in the matter, you know. You don't have to sit around waiting to get *picked*."

Janine blew her nose into the cheerfully colored cocktail napkin. "What do you suggest I do, then?"

"Well . . . you need to go from being someone who is picked to someone who is the picker."

She looked at me with a blank expression that I knew was a mask for skepticism, maybe even hostility. Her nose was orange from the napkin, adding to the confusion of makeup on her face. I have never been the expert on dating, and Janine knew it.

"You could . . . you could go online."

"I've tried that before," Janine said. "All I got were liars, freaks, and perverts. One guy demanded that I take a genetic test. He brought a kit to our first date! He was adopted and wanted to make sure we weren't related. He stopped calling when I refused. Another one wanted me to invest in his stupid start-up. That one stopped calling after I told him that I didn't have the money. The last one took me to a fancy restaurant, ordered us drinks and appetizers. We both had steaks, and I thought things were going okay—not great but okay."

"And?"

"And he excused himself to use the men's room and never came back. He stiffed me with the bill. Dined and dashed."

"That's criminal!"

"I felt so pathetic sitting there waiting for him, making excuses to the waitress about how he wasn't feeling well. That dinner was the last straw. No more online dating."

"It's just bad luck."

Janine sighed. "I don't want to be old and alone."

"Nobody does," I said. It was disheartening to hear Janine like this. She was usually all about partying and being single and independent.

"I don't know what to do anymore," she said. "Join a commune? Or a cult?"

"You shouldn't give up on online dating so soon. Everyone's doing it. When you tried it, it wasn't as popular as it is now." Janine was an early adopter. She got her first date on Match.com before I even had email. "It seems like everyone finds their mate online these days. Just look at the wedding announcements in the paper. Last Sunday, there were three couples who met on setmeup.com."

"If everyone does it, why don't you?"

This is what drives me crazy about Janine. She's always trying to drag me into her world.

"We aren't talking about me, remember?"

"We *never* talk about you. And it's not because I'm always talking about me. You hate talking about you. Why is that?"

"Are those margaritas making you nasty? Because I don't—"

"I'm not trying to be nasty. I'm just asking a question."

"A nasty question."

"There's nothing nasty about it. You just told me that you thought online dating is such a great thing. Then why don't you do it?"

"Maybe because I'm not looking for anyone."

"That's bullshit."

"It is not!"

"You're either lying to me or to yourself. Either way, it's not the truth."

Maybe it's because Janine and I have been friends since junior high, but whenever we argue, we end up sounding like twelve-year-olds.

"You have a problem with the truth, you know. Sometimes."

"I do not."

"Have you told your mom yet?"

She was talking about my pending divorce, which was now three months from being official. I took a long sip of margarita in response. Janine knew she was pushing it. I had explained to her that it would be too difficult for Ahma to understand. There is too much stigma associated with divorce for Koreans of my mother's generation. It would be too shameful for her to tell her friends the news. It would be too traumatic after my father's death. So I told her that Louis and I were separated. Separated meant there was still hope. It meant that we still loved each other, that we were trying to work things out. But Ahma saw through my lies, as she always did. "*You* the liar," she had said to me, fixing me with that slo-mo look. But that was all she had said. I didn't ask her what she meant, and she didn't say it expressly. Neither one of us mentioned the *D* word—*divorce*—so both of us could continue pretending. I could pretend that she didn't really know, and she could pretend that I was going to stay married. Who said I wasn't my mother's daughter?

"You have to tell her sometime," Janine said. "I never understood what happened with you and Louis. I mean, he's a pretty decent guy. For a guy. It's not like you fought or that he turned out to be a freak of nature like Megan's husband."

Megan was a friend of ours from high school. I guess we three formed a clique, except she considered herself a tad better than me and Janine. And to be honest, she was. She was taller than me and thinner than Janine, and she had a boyfriend who qualified as a hottie. She had sex with him the summer after junior year. That would have made her a slut if the other kids had found out about it, but he never talked, and neither did Janine or I, except to each other. We were a bit awed by Megan's nonvirgin status, Janine enviously and I fearfully so. It was as though she turned into a werewolf at night. She looked so normal! Just the same as before she'd done "it." Anyway, she and I lost touch when I went away to college, but I get regular updates from Janine, who still talks to her every once in a while.

"Can you imagine? He was IM'ing teenage boys, from work! X-rated porno messages. So now, Megan is in the process of filing a messy divorce, although it sounds like she's more upset that he lost his job than that he's a pedophile."

"He is so lucky that they didn't call the cops."

"Maybe they should have," Janine said. "I mean, he's probably going to do it again, even though he swears up and down that he won't. I told her that she should force him to see a therapist as part of the settlement."

"You can't trust anybody."

Janine gave me a look that made her seem almost sober. "Was there something *funny* about Louis?"

"No. No! Nothing at all. The most normal guy in the world . . . I mean, nice and everything, and even good in bed . . . good, but not crazy. Nothing strange like *that*."

"God, you were so lucky. That's all I'm looking for. Someone normal. The good-in-bed part is just a huge bonus."

She looked so depressed that I let my guard down. "Yeah, me too."

One thing I can say for Janine is that she makes a quick recovery. In an instant, her features lifted and her eyes brightened. "Aha! You admitted it. You're a hypocrite. You want me to do it, but you think you're too good for online dating."

"Not true!"

"Prove it."

So we made a pact. We would both post our profiles on setmeup. com. It would be something we would do together.

~

To be perfectly honest, I've toyed with the idea of signing up with setmeup.com ever since Louis and I separated. I often wondered how I would fare with just a thumbnail photo and a few lines to capture someone's attention. But, like most things, it wasn't something that I actually had the courage to do, for a lot of different reasons. Mostly, I was afraid that someone I knew would find me on the site, which was a bit illogical since almost everyone but Ahma knows that I'm single again.

But after my conversation with Janine, I wonder, What *is* there to be afraid of? If someone sees my profile, what are they going to do?

Laugh at me? Think that I'm pathetic because I need to advertise for dates? I'm not any less pathetic because I don't advertise for dates and instead sit home alone, binge-watching shows on Netflix. Besides, anyone who finds my profile on setmeup would be trolling for dates, too, so what's the big deal? We would be in the same club.

What I don't want is to sign up, have my pathetic self out there for all the world to see, let everyone know that what I want is a mate . . . and then end up with nothing. Nobody. But the odds of meeting my soul mate through friends, coworkers, or a random encounter are miniscule, especially the random-encounter odds, since I don't go anywhere except El Toreador, and then always with Janine. I could meet a lot more men through setmeup.com than I ever could through friends or acquaintances. The numbers work out in favor of setmeup.com. Maybe *that* is the real issue. When I told Janine that I wasn't interested in meeting anyone, she accused me of hiding from the truth, of breaking Rule #1. But maybe it is the truth—or at least something resembling the truth. I do want a man—just not any man. I want Louis, or the life I had with him. I don't want to be divorced. I don't want to come home to a dark house. Of course, I can't tell Janine this. I can barely admit it to myself. Comfort isn't the same thing as romance. Familiarity isn't the same thing as passion. I know I should expect more. Shouldn't I?

The next day, Janine calls me when I'm in my car on the way home from running errands.

"I already got six emails. Three of them look good. I'm going to meet one of them Monday after work."

"You're not going for drinks . . ."

"No, coffee. He doesn't drink."

"Sounds promising."

"He skis. He surfs. He's thirty-five."

"Too young."

"Only three years younger than me."

"Four."

"Right. Four."

For some reason, Janine's last birthday hasn't quite stuck, even though she's had plenty of time to get used to it. She turned thirty-nine eight months ago.

"His picture looks really cute. He's six feet tall."

"What does he do?"

"He's an astronaut."

I almost rear-end the car in front of me. Astronauts are posting their profiles on setmeup? The car behind me honks.

"And he plays the guitar."

"He sounds perfect."

"Yeah, I know." Janine sighs dreamily.

"Listen, I got to go. I'm hitting a lot of traffic."

Forty minutes later, I am sitting in front of my computer creating a profile on setmeup.com. I type in my birth date, name, and email address. Should I create a fake ID? Oh, what the hell. I change my birth date by a couple of months. I try to create an email account, but all the Alice Chang IDs are taken. I think about using a phony name, but that doesn't seem like a good way to start a relationship, virtual or not. Be brave, be honest, be true . . . I settle for Alice_AliceChang@mailme.com. Height. Five four. Okay, it's probably closer to five three, but that sounds so . . . short. Anyway, what's a guy going to do, measure me on our first date? Body type. Slender? Average? *Slender* sounds too svelte, and *average* seems to mean dumpy. Deciding that in this case, less is more, I click "Slender" and vow to lose five pounds, just to keep it honest. Eye color. Brown. Or is it black? It's really dark brown, but that's not an option. I click on "Black" because brown sounds too light, even though black sounds like an exaggeration. Hair color. Dark brown is an option here, and while it's factually accurate, I don't think it's the right choice. Dark brown is really brunette, and Asians aren't brunettes, no matter how light their hair color. People generally think of Asian hair as black, even if it's really brown or dark brown with red highlights after a SoCal summer.

My hair isn't the same color as Janine's bottled-black shade—I think it's called jet black (she's naturally a mousy brown)—but selecting "Black" for hair color makes the most sense, so I do. Next is "Body art." I had pierced ears at one time, but they closed up years ago. I click "None."

Now I have to describe my "best-case scenario for a date." The website helpfully suggests possible responses like "white-water rafting" or "sushi and a movie." I try to think of something more creative but can't, so I go with "sushi and a movie." Next, it's "Name your best feature." The only options pertain to body parts. What about sparkling wit? Intelligence? I guess those aren't features. Anyway, who really cares about those? It's a brave new visually oriented world. I click on "Butt" because it's true, but then I immediately regret it. What if I get ass fetishists? Guys who are obsessed with anal sex? But "butt" really is the honest answer. It's certainly not my belly or chest or lips. Too flabby, too flat, too dry and thin. My arms and legs are okay, but I wouldn't consider them my best feature, since they're just arms and legs—nothing special, although they work. At one point, I might have clicked on "Hair," but the wiry gray strands that rise from my scalp like cobras have got me in a serious funk. My butt isn't quite as perky as it once was, but I value it for what it isn't yet—too flabby, too flat, too wide, too wobbly. Maybe next year I'll have to create a new profile if my butt, too, succumbs to gravitational pull.

Do I really want to be doing this? Grading my body parts for the highest bidder? Now comes the sneaky part. Status. "Single," "Separated," "Divorced," "Widowed," and "Other." At least they have the decency not to have "Married" as an option. I guess that's what "Other" means— "Married but cheating," or it could mean "In a relationship but thinking about leaving." I briefly consider clicking "Widowed," rationalizing that my marriage died, our love died. But did it really? Is that why I have this heavy lump in my throat and a pain in my stomach? Louis accused me of being indifferent to our relationship. If I were truly indifferent, wouldn't that mean I would be over this by now? He obviously is, if his globe-trotting, career makeover, and new relationship are any indication. I click on "Divorced" because I don't think anything will change in the next three months, and that seems closer to the truth now than "Separated." One small click for reality, one giant click for Alice.

Next comes the hardest part. "Describe yourself in 50 words or less." I tap my fingers lightly on the keyboard, feeling like a sprinter waiting for the starting gun. Fifty words or less . . . finally, I settle on "Looking to hang out with someone who appreciates good coffee, freshly baked bread, and engaging conversation." I might as well have written, "Boring woman looking for boring man." I hit the "Complete" button before I can change my mind, click "I agree" to the terms of the setmeup.com website agreement, and then wait until I get the message, "CONGRATULATIONS AND WELCOME TO SETMEUP.COM!"

Now comes the fun part—I get to create a setmeup "wish list." I'm **F** seeking **M** ages **35** to **45**. One click of the mouse, and boom! Fifty pages of eligible men. At ten profiles per page, that's five hundred eligible men *in my zip code*! I would have never guessed it. Where are they all hiding? Where do they do their grocery shopping? Literally hundreds of single men in my neighborhood. Wow! Who knew? I browse through the listings. The men come in all shapes and sizes. I realize that more than a few of them are wearing baseball caps, which I construe as a bad-faith attempt to conceal a receding hairline. Many of them have posted pictures of themselves outdoors, wearing shorts and weighted down by oppressive-looking backpacks. Some of the pictures look disturbingly like mug shots. A couple of deranged-looking men have taken pictures of themselves shirtless, flaunting their hirsute chest and bellies. Are they trying to prove their virility? Or are they just being honest about their flaws up front?

Nearly all the men are looking for women younger than they are. A few give the upper limit at forty. No man is looking for a woman more than two years older than he is. One man, John431, age forty-six, is looking for "a long-term relationship, possibly marriage" with a woman eighteen to twenty-five. Eighteen?

There are two ways to find a perfect setmeup on setmeup.com. You can post your profile, with a picture, and wait for someone to notice you. Or, you can adopt the "take your life in your own hands" approach and send an email yourself. While I would never approach a man in a bar, being online makes me feel braver. A handful of men describe themselves as "nice guys": "The last nice guy in Southern California . . ." "A nice guy who is looking for a serious relationship . . ." "A nice guy who wants to meet someone . . ." I like nice guys but am a little leery of men who describe themselves as nice guys. Who says? Can I ask your last girlfriend? I exclude the long-bearded fellas, the fatty good old boys, the guys who look like they've spent the last few years in state prison, and the ones who are clearly insane, illiterate, or perverted ("The Lord hath ordered all Christian men to find theeselves womin . . ." "Firehorse looking for love-fire for me . . ." "I love food and fun and GOOD SERVICE for delicious taste . . ."). I also eliminate the ones who obviously can't spell ("Funny, outgoing, inteligint . . ." "Loves movies, dansing, moonliting . . .") but not the merely typo-prone ("Nice guys looking for someone with whom I can . . ." "Enjoy hiking, biking, swimmingg and . . ."), since that would eliminate virtually all of them. Out of the five hundred men, I have narrowed my list down to . . . seven. From that seven, I pick two: "Nice guy looking for partner," even though I'm suspicious of nice guys, and "Enjoys hiking, picnics, and good conversation." I consider adding "Food and wine lover looking for someone who enjoys life . . ." but fear that could be code for "Fat alcoholic hedonist looking for same." Maybe when I get a little more comfortable with this whole online-dating scene, I'll be less suspicious and give "Food and wine lover" a chance if he's still available.

So, now I have two potential setmeups. I can either send them an email and start a conversation, or I can take the chickenshit approach and send them a "smile." The smile lets them know I'm interested and invites them to check out my profile. If they're interested in me, then they can email me. It's a more passive approach, but the rejection is milder. I take the chickenshit approach. I send my two smiles and then, to stop myself from obsessively checking my email, I log out of the computer. I even go so far as to switch off the surge protector. The whole machine noisily shuts down, and all the bleeping lights extinguish.

I haven't had a date, a real date, for about . . . twenty years. I can't believe it, but it's true. I met Louis when I was eighteen. Suddenly I remember the two of us, sitting at a coffeehouse on campus, studying for an anthropology final. We are drinking cappuccinos and sharing a piece of shortbread the size of a brick. He saves the last bite for me, even though I know that he wants it.

I can still feel the smooth wood bench underneath my khaki shorts, smell the bitter espresso, taste the buttery shortbread. A tear slips down my cheek, and then a couple more, but I don't wipe them away, afraid that if I move, the memory will disappear like a startled rabbit down a hole.

Nice Guy emails me first: Thanks for smiling at me. I'm not exactly sure how this works, since I just signed on with this service. Do you want to meet for coffee?

Getting coffee seems to be the activity of choice for setmeup first dates. It's safer—less chance of someone slipping you a drug and carrying you out the door claiming that you're drunk. Less time consuming, in case the date turns out to be a complete bust, and if it turns out to be a good time, you can always linger or move on to dinner. *Date progression*, Janine calls it. You start small and then build up if it looks promising. Kind of like buying a starter home, I guess. I email Nice Guy back: Coffee sounds great.

Later that evening, Nice Guy emails me with three choices for dates and times at Spilled Beans in Brea, written as though they are answers to a multiple-choice question.

I pick (c), I write, which is Sunday afternoon—tomorrow—at three o'clock.

I don't expect him to write back, but he does. I look forward to meeting you.

Polite, and he writes in full sentences.

CHAPTER EIGHT

I posted the best picture of myself I could find, but now I'm worried that Nice Guy is going to expect me to be better looking and thinner than I am. I don't have the shiny jet-black sheet of hair that Asian women are famous for—my hair is wavy and more dark mahogany than black as I rapidly descend into middle age and lose my pigmentation along with my jawline. I haven't put on a pair of real running shoes since the turn of the century. I've started to develop a slight bra over-hang, and the twin peaks inside that bra are looking more like melting glaciers. And don't get me started on the pillowy softness of my belly and the age spots that have started to appear on my neck. I get onto the floor right then and there and start to do a hundred sit-ups. I stop at ten and take a breather. I wiggle my way up to ten more sit-ups with the help of my hands on my knees, then spring up from the floor like a ninja before crashing back down on my rear like the out-of-shape klutz that I am. Now, time for a nutritious fiber-filled breakfast.

An hour before my scheduled date, Janine calls.

"Are you checking up on me?"

"Yes. Are you nervous?"

"No, it's just coffee."

She cackles. "What are you wearing?"

"Pink lace undies with ruffles, why do you ask?"

She laughs again. "You are on edge!"

"What do you expect? I'm going on my first date in twenty years."

"I know. That's why I'm calling."

"Thanks for the support."

"Don't forget to ask if he has any hot friends."

"That'll be the first thing out of my mouth."

I hang up before she can say anything else.

I won't even bother describing the numerous outfit changes. Let's just say that I end up wearing the first outfit I tried on and leave the mess in my room for later.

It is two fifty-five when I get to Spilled Beans. Two fifty-eight. I check my lipstick in the rearview mirror. Exactly where I left it, on my lips. I check my teeth. Why does my skin look so bad in the rearview mirror? Every line is magnified. Is this really how others see me in the cruel glare of sunlight? Maybe I should move to Seattle. Three oh one. I get out of the car. I take a deep breath.

I walk up to the counter, pretending I'm just here to get a coffee, as though I need the caffeine. My palms are sweating, and I feel light headed. I pay for my coffee and look around, feeling the heat from the paper cup warm my hand. A couple of college students, or are they high schoolers? I can't tell anymore. An old man reading the newspaper. For a minute, my heart stops. But that can't be him. Mr. Nice Guy posted his picture. I avoid eye contact, just in case. I head for the only empty table and notice a man sitting alone at a table outside. We make eye contact. He smiles. I smile back. He points to himself and then to me, meaning *Should I come to your table?* I shake my head and point to myself and then to his table. I walk outside, trying not to spill my drink, trying not to look nervous, trying to be perfect.

He stands up as I approach, a gesture that I simultaneously appreciate and hate because it's polite but draws attention to us. It also makes me feel feeble.

"Alice?"

"Hi."

"I'm Rick." He pulls out a chair for me, and I sit. He is better looking than in his profile photo. He has thick, closely cropped dark-brown hair with flecks of gray, dark-brown eyes, and a strong jaw.

"Have you been waiting long?" I ask, and then I pray that he didn't notice me pull up, didn't see me sit inside my car and check my lipstick and my teeth.

"No, not at all."

I notice that he is not eating or drinking anything. I realize that he was waiting for me before he ordered. I look guiltily at my coffee.

He stands. He is tall, at least a couple of inches over six feet. He is broad in the chest and trim in the waist. His jeans fit well. "Do you want anything else?"

The *else* makes me blush. I shake my head. What is a man like this doing on an online-dating site? Why isn't he already married to a former supermodel, with three gorgeous kids and a McMansion in the suburbs?

He returns holding a cappuccino in one hand and a giant chocolate chip cookie in the other. He breaks it in two and offers half to me. Is this some kind of test? Is he checking to see whether I'm a dieting freak? A no-carb kind of gal? Or is he just being polite, and really what he wants is to scarf the whole cookie by himself?

I take the cookie and place it on the napkin that he was thoughtful enough to bring. If he really didn't want to share his cookie with me, he wouldn't have brought two napkins, now, would he?

He is looking at me expectantly. Did I miss a question?

"Excuse me?"

He is looking at the crumbled mess on my napkin. I've been playing with my food.

"I guess I'm nervous."

He smiles and my stomach wraps around itself. "I guess you haven't done this before."

I feel my face get hot again. I am having a hard time paying attention to what he is saying. "Excuse me?"

"Online dating, I mean."

I take a sip of coffee and glance around. He laughs. I swallow hard and drop a few crumbs into my mouth.

I learn that Rick is an architect with his own firm, that he likes to travel, and that he is forty-one years old. He was born in a suburb of Chicago but spent much of his childhood traveling and living in Haiti, Mexico, and the Philippines, all places where he has family. His upbringing sounds complicated and incredibly glamorous and worldly compared to my boring, stable one. He attended boarding school in England as a teenager and architecture school in California, where he met his wife. His marriage ended in divorce about six months ago (no kids), and he is just now ready to start dating.

Janine says that a good coffee date is supposed to lead to dinner. Rick stands up at four o'clock and mentions that he has to be some-where, which tells me something. It doesn't matter. By the end of the hour, I am exhausted from the effort of trying to be good enough. My mouth hurts from smiling, and I have a slight headache. I call Janine as soon as I get into the car, and we meet at El Toreador later that evening.

"So?" she asks, a sly look on her face, as though expecting to hear that I am planning to run off with my new setmeup.

I sit down in the booth across from her. In between bites of chips and sips of margarita, I tell her everything I know about him. She smiles dreamily.

"When are you going to see him again?"

"Probably never." I take another swig of my drink and pull it closer to my side of the table.

She narrows her eyes and leans across the table so that her shirt gapes open like a yawn. "You don't sound thrilled. His background sounds amazing, and I thought you said he was hot."

"He's good looking, yeah. Amazing, really."

"Then what?"

"I don't think we hit it off."

"What do you mean?"

"Just that. We didn't hit it off. I mean, he was perfectly nice, but I'm here and not at dinner with him."

"Did you have stuff to talk about, or were there awkward silences?"

"We talked the whole time."

"Did he look bored?"

"I'm not sure."

"Did he make eye contact? Did he pay attention when you were talking?"

I remember his dark-brown eyes looking into mine. My stomach does a somersault just thinking about it.

"I guess."

"It's the usual Alice thing. You just have no grip on reality."

"What are you talking about?"

"You haven't been on a date in nearly two decades! I'm telling you, I've been in the trenches. It's not easy and it's not fun. And he sounds like someone you made up."

"I didn't make him up."

"I know you didn't. What I mean is that he sounds great. It sounds like a perfect date."

"It was a perfectly fine date. We just had coffee."

"You have no idea how lucky you got. Your first setmeup, and you don't get a pervert or someone who is six inches shorter than his profile. The fact that he resembles his profile picture is amazing!"

"He actually looks better than his profile picture. But I seriously doubt that he's going to call. He's out of my league."

"Have you even looked at yourself in the mirror? Do you even know what you look like? I think you're just afraid of being in a relationship. You're afraid of rejection, and you're afraid of making yourself emotionally vulnerable."

I cringe and hunch my shoulders. Fortunately, the music is loud and nobody can hear us.

"Don't you want to be in a relationship?"

I shrug. "I don't know."

"It's hard to tell with you, Alice. Sometimes I just don't know."

"Why? Because I'm not talking about getting married to someone I just met?"

"He checks all the boxes."

"I don't have a checklist."

"You know what I mean."

"Anyway, he's too good to be true."

She furrows her eyebrows suspiciously. "Do you think he was lying? That he's one of those online scam artists, like that guy I met who dined and ditched me?"

"I don't think so. But maybe. I mean, why else would he be on an online-dating site?"

"What do you mean?"

"There must be something wrong with him."

"Alice! *You're* on an online-dating site. *I'm* on an online-dating site! You told me to do it."

"Yeah, but that's different."

"Why? How?"

I look at her, and she is glaring at me. "There's a difference," I say slowly, reminding myself to tread lightly here—minefields abound.

"Yeah, and what's that?" Her nostrils are slightly flared, and her face is flushed.

"You know what I mean."

"The problem is, I do know what you mean, Alice. You think I need to be on a dating website and you don't. You're just doing it for me."

"Listen, you are making too big of a deal of this."

Janine takes a long slurp of her margarita. No, wait, that's my margarita, but I don't care. I just want to go home.

"You have no idea how hard it is to be your friend sometimes."

"No, I guess I didn't know that it was so hard to be my friend."

"Sometimes I feel like the main reason we're friends is so that you can feel better by comparing yourself to me."

"How can you say such a thing?"

She shrugs and takes another sip of my margarita.

"It's true, isn't it?" she says. "I'm your pathetic single friend. The one who will probably never get married. Don't think I can't tell."

This conversation has veered into dangerous self-pitying, drunken territory.

"If you felt so resentful, why didn't you say anything earlier?"

"And hear you deny everything? That's the thing about you, Alice. You don't say anything. But you're not fooling anybody."

"I'm not trying to fool anyone!"

"Only yourself. Remember that night at Megan's? The summer before you left for college?"

It was the night my former prom date aurally treated everyone to his deflowering.

"You don't have to bring that up . . ."

"Jim was screwing that girl from Saint Vincent's, and everyone at the party could hear them? And he was *your* boyfriend, and you didn't do anything about it!"

"He wasn't my boyfriend. We just went to the prom together. I even told you that back then."

Janine's features harden. Her pity has vanished, and in its place is contempt. "You know what I'm talking about."

"I really don't want to talk about that. What's the point?"

"What's the point?"

"I really wasn't upset. I felt weird because everyone was looking at me, but you were more upset about it than I was."

I can still hear Janine banging on the locked bedroom door. Her cries echoed down the stairs, *"Open the door, you asshole! Open the goddamned door!"* I remember Jim's best friends, Walter and Greg, snickering and elbowing each other. Still, the moans from the bedroom didn't stop.

"You know *why* I was upset?" Janine asks. I shake my head and reach for my purse, but she grabs my wrist and forces me to look into her eyes. "You broke the Number One Friendship Rule."

"So did you."

"You broke it first. You knew I had a crush on him even before he asked you out. I told you how excited I was when he told me he wanted to talk to me about something important. You remember?"

I *do* remember. She had thought he might ask her to the Homecoming Dance. I remember that she wore her best jeans and freshened up her shiny pink lip gloss before meeting him at the football field after school. But instead of asking her to the dance, he asked her whether she thought I would go with him. I still remember her face when she told me afterward, her smile wide and stiff, her voice loud with forced excitement. I felt the effort she was making to hide her disappointment. I can still see the contorted expression on her face as she said, "I can't believe I thought he was actually going to ask me. Who would want to ask fat, zitty Janine?" Then she laughed as though her feelings weren't hurt at all, and instead of putting my arms around her like I wanted and telling her how beautiful she was and saying, *Screw him—we'll stay home and watch a movie on my parents' new VCR,* I laughed along with her and then told her to tell him yes, I would go with him.

"You knew that I hooked up with him later, at the end of the year," she says. "You knew it then, and you never said anything. You knew that's why I was so upset that night. I wasn't upset for you. It was because I thought he liked *me.*"

I shake my head and try to leave, but she won't let go of my wrist, won't stop talking. I always suspected it, but I was never actually sure.

"We've never talked about that," she says. "It just sat there between us, and I always felt bad about it."

"It doesn't matter. It was a long time ago. I really don't care. Not then and not now."

She breathes out sharply through her nose and drops my wrist. "That's exactly what I mean. You make everyone else put themselves out there, but you play your cards close to the vest. Is that what you're afraid of with this guy? Having to take an emotional risk? To actually be open enough to be in a real relationship?"

"What are you talking about?"

"Or is it that you don't want to be like me?"

"You've had too much to drink."

"You're being dishonest. You know what I'm talking about. You just want me to say it so you can deny everything and make me look like the bad guy, the petty friend who is always bringing up the past. You won't even try to meet me halfway, will you? No wonder Louis left you."

That's hitting below the belt. I can forgive her for messing around with Jim from high school and for insulting me, but even I have my limits. I grab my purse and toss a twenty on the table, which more than covers my margarita and share of the chips.

"Listen, I didn't mean that . . ."

But I'm not in the mood for half-assed apologies.

The tears start only after I leave the El Toreador parking lot, when I am safely on the road and driving away from the explosion that just shattered what I thought was a friendship. I wipe them away as quickly as they come, determined not to let Janine's words get the better of me.

I am thankful that Ahma is not home. I pull my carcass into the house, head up the stairs, and flop onto my bed. I try not to think about what's just happened, but Janine's words repeat themselves. Suddenly, I want to speak with Louis. I dial his number, but he is not there. I leave a message: "Hi, Louis. It's me. Just wanted to check in and see how you were doing. Hope you're doing well. Talk to you soon."

I feel alone and abandoned. I want to talk to somebody, anybody. Anybody, that is, but Ahma. The last thing I want to hear is the sound of the key turning in the lock in the front door.

I hear her footsteps, the sound of shoes being removed.

"Alice?"

I hold my breath. Of course she knows I'm home. My car is in the driveway. This is her house. I have no right to privacy here. I should come out, let her see my reddened face and my puffy eyes. Instead, I pretend to be asleep. I hear Ahma puttering around in the kitchen, emptying out the dishwasher, which I neglected to do. I crawl underneath the covers, still fully dressed, and turn out the lights.

CHAPTER NINE

To my surprise, Rick calls me Tuesday, a couple of days after our coffee date, as I am driving to Restin. The conversation is brief, since we are both on the freeway. After dispensing with the necessary formalities, he asks, "Do you want to go to the zoo this weekend?"

"The zoo?"

"Yeah, I haven't been in years, and I thought it might be fun."

We make plans to meet in front of the gorilla cage at 2:00 p.m. on Saturday, and then I quickly hang up because I need to pay attention to driving in this stop-and-go traffic. With my hands free, my mind can wander. Why the zoo? Why late afternoon instead of brunch or dinner? Why the gorilla cage? I have the urge to talk to Janine—she would certainly have some interesting theories—but I am no longer on speaking terms with her. Remembering my falling out with my former best friend dampens the thrill of receiving my first "callback." But still I wonder—why another afternoon date? Am I not good enough for a *real* date—am I not a "dinner and a movie" kind of gal? And why oh why the gorilla cage instead of the cuddly pandas, the regal lions, or the beautiful and elegant flamingos?

~

The Restin Public Library has been on a spending spree because some rich woman died and left it a million dollars. I had assumed that she was the wife of a real estate developer or an investment banker, but during our lunch break, Bertha informs me that the rich woman was a *maid* who used to bring her daughter to the library so that she could get the education she wasn't receiving in the Santa Ana public schools. This woman cleaned the houses of wealthy people in Restin but somehow managed to save a million bucks to donate to the library!

"Why didn't she leave the money to her daughter?" I wonder aloud.

"She didn't need to, I guess. Her daughter got a free ride to Harvard and became a heart surgeon. I heard she lives in Newport Beach." Bertha laughs. "I guess all those afternoons at the library was time well spent." She takes another sip of Diet Coke and shoves a handful of chips into her mouth. "Kind of makes you feel like a slacker, huh?"

I know that by "you" she actually means "us," but I can't help feeling insulted, and with good reason. Out there, house cleaners are leaving million-dollar donations to public institutions. Out there, daughters of house cleaners are getting full scholarships to Harvard and becoming surgeons. In here, a library staffer is struggling to lose weight while munching on junk food and soda. In here, a college-educated woman, a former math prodigy, raised in a two-parent household in a good school district and therefore lacking any excuses, is barely cobbling together a living while sleeping in her childhood bedroom, waiting for her divorce to become final, and mooching off her mother.

"Is Mr. Park in today?" I ask. It's only been a few days, and I don't expect him to have translated much. Still, maybe he can tell me what the notebook is, even if he can't tell me everything it says. I don't want to be pushy, but I hope he'll mention it when he sees me.

"You mean Sam? Yeah, he's around. He's been busy all morning with emergencies. He's probably in the courtyard, de-stressing with tai chi."

I still can't get used to calling Mr. Park by his first name. It seems against the laws of nature, even though I know that Mr. Park wouldn't be offended—at least I don't think so. I find it hard to believe that any Korean man of my parents' generation doesn't harbor a teeny bit of disdain for the lack of manners and sheer ignorance of the Korean American youth—even those of us who are not exactly youthful anymore.

In the courtyard, I find Mr. Park standing on one leg, the other leg bent into a triangle with his foot pressed against the inner part of the standing leg. His hands are clasped, palms together, and his eyes are closed. I have the strange sensation that I am spying on him. I don't want to interrupt. I'll ask him about the notebook later. He probably hasn't had a chance to work on it yet anyway.

I hurriedly turn around and leave the courtyard area. Everyone knows that Mr. Park does tai chi, but he seemed to be doing something else. He seemed to be praying.

Religion was a topic that always made me feel uncomfortable growing up. My mother took me to church when I was younger, but I always had the feeling it was more for the socializing than the enlightening. I never understood a word of the sermons and found the whole experience a little scary, to tell the truth. The reverend made little moaning sounds, like he was crying, and sometimes he would burst out wailing. Other members of the congregation would join him in making the same kind of awful crying and wailing noises. One time, a group of people got up and made some sort of communal confession of their sins—I couldn't understand what they were saying, but I got the general idea that they were coming clean to God about something, or else asking him for something that they really, really wanted. Then they all started wailing and moaning and crying—it was like a scene out of *The Exorcist*. Afterward, when I asked my mom what all that was about, she gave a little laugh and said, "That's just how Koreans pray." One of the sinners was Mrs. Choi, a friend of my mom's. She came over the following week with a large half-filled box of peaches—my mom and her friends were always buying jumbo boxes of something and sharing the excess—and she seemed perfectly normal.

It wasn't just the drama at church that got to me. It was also the drama before church. My father flat-out stated that he didn't believe in Jesus Christ. Whenever he said this, my mother would say, "Ohmana, Ohmana, Ohmana," which is the Korean equivalent of "Oh my God!" This was the only time my parents ever argued. My mom would hurl threats at him on behalf of our heavenly creator, things like, "Bad luck will fall on us because of your stubborn lack of faith!" and "Your dental practice will be in danger if you have no blessings from God!" My father would yell back, "Just because you go to church doesn't mean that you are better than everyone else!" My mother would snap at me to get my shoes on, and we would make the forty-minute drive to the church in Cerritos. The only good thing about church was that after service, they served salty tripe soup with kimchi and soft, chewy glazed doughnuts.

Funny enough, my father never allowed me to stay home from church. Maybe he wanted to preserve the one day a week when he had the whole house to himself. But he wasn't a nonbeliever. He believed in Buddha and reincarnation and the sayings of Confucius. In a way, he believed in Christ too—he believed that Christ was Buddha was Muhammad was the will of the people. "Everyone needs to believe in God," he said. "Your mother thinks I don't believe in God, but I do. I probably believe in God more than she does." I'm still not sure what he meant by that.

Ahma doesn't go to church anymore. She stopped going when I was in high school. I wonder what happened to Mrs. Choi. She and my mother are no longer friends.

~

Usually I'm in Restin all day on Thursdays, but this week I have to leave early to drive down to Long Beach. Harry Gee is on vacation for the next two weeks, and I need to make sure that the bills are paid and payroll is met in his absence. I still haven't had a chance to talk to Mr. Park—he was in another meeting when I stopped by his office today—so now I have to wait until next Tuesday. It's only been a week, and he's probably been so busy he hasn't had time to start translating my father's notebook. He warned me that it would take some time, so I have to be patient. My phone rings as soon as I get in my car. Janine's name shows up on the screen. I let it go to voice mail.

Friday is a slow day at work, and I leave Randolph Johnson's office early. I've received a few emails from potential setmeups but haven't bothered responding to them. Instead, I spend the evening deep-conditioning my hair and giving myself a manicure.

Finally it is Saturday afternoon, and I am standing in front of the gorilla enclosure at 1:55 p.m. Children swarm around me while moms and dads wearing baseball caps and shorts carry giant pretzels and juice boxes. I feel adrift and self-conscious—not as conspicuous as, say, sitting alone at a bar, but misplaced nonetheless, as though I took a wrong turn on the freeway and ended up here, instead of the South Coast Plaza. Where are my children? Why don't I have a chubby-cheeked daughter carrying a churro, or a freckle-faced son darting around to get a better glimpse of the gorillas? Why don't I have a baseball-cap-wearing husband with skinny legs? How did I end up here alone?

And then I see Rick, trotting around the corner, exactly on time, for it's now precisely 2:00 p.m. He is wearing jeans and a cotton T-shirt that shows off nicely (but not overly) muscled arms.

"Didn't mean to keep you waiting," he says, and I burst into tears.

My sudden outburst attracts curious stares, and I am so mortified that I consider climbing over the fence separating us from the gorillas and letting them finish me off. Instead, I let Rick lead me over to a quiet spot under a leafy tree and wipe the tears streaming down my cheeks. He doesn't say anything, which compels me to explain.

"My father died," I say. His eyes widen. "No, not today—a few months ago, in April. I was just remembering coming here with him." Maybe it's the truth. Maybe, instead of a family to take to the zoo, all I want is someone to take *me* to the zoo. Maybe I just want to eat churros and look at gorillas and have someone else drive for once.

"Do you want to go home?" he asks.

I shake my head.

"Do you want to see the lions?"

That is exactly what I want.

I have been to this zoo about twenty times, but the last time was about ten years ago. We manage to catch up with a free guided tour and learn all sorts of interesting animal trivia. Did you know that the polar bear's fur is not really white? It only looks white because it reflects the surrounding snow. Did you know a rhino's horn is made of the same material as human hair? Did you know that owls have asymmetric ears so that they can hear noises in the sky as well as on the ground? Macaws mate for life, the guide tells us, and I purposely avoid Rick's eyes. Giraffes' tongues are purplish black to protect against sunburn.

"All these adaptations have a purpose," the zoo guide informs us.

Four giraffes are gathered on a dirt platform, next to a two-foot-deep ditch and surrounded by a four-foot-high wall.

"Can't the giraffes simply step over the barrier?" Rick asks.

The guide nods. "Yes. It's not the wall that contains them. The ditch is a psychological barrier. The giraffes don't like to step down, so even though they could easily climb into the ditch and over the fence, they don't because they can't see what's down below. Once one of our giraffes got spooked by a red balloon and escaped. Her fear of the balloon was greater than her fear of falling. It took a while to get her back where she belonged."

I look carefully at the giraffes. I guess even psychological barriers have their limitations.

We walk over to the marabou stork, which might just be the ugliest creature in the zoo. It has a scabby head with a shriveled air sac that resembles what I imagine an old man's testicles look like. The guide explains that the carrion-eating bird's head is bald so that it can stick it into dead animals without collecting too much bacteria. I glance over at Rick.

"Hungry?" he asks with a grin.

In fact, I am. It's nearly six o'clock. We decide that rather than eating at Nairobi Village, the zoo's only decent restaurant, we are both in the mood for sushi. Since we drove separately, Rick walks me to my car, and there is an awkward moment, at least in my mind, where I wonder if he is going to kiss me. Instead, he says, "See you in a few minutes," and I get in the car feeling a little foolish. Do I want him to kiss me? Do I like him? I think so. Besides being gorgeous, he's kind and patient. He didn't freak out when I started crying. He didn't try to cut our date short when I told him about my dad. It might have been too much for some guys, especially for a second date. I guess I am waiting to see how he feels about me before I decide how I feel about him. Whether and how much I like him depends on whether and how much he likes me.

I pull into the parking lot of Zen Sushi, guessing that I have arrived before Rick. I sit in my car for a few minutes, figuring it's better to wait in my car than in a crowded restaurant. I see a black Aston Martin Roadster pull into a parking space, and I am surprised when Rick steps out of it. Watching him as a stranger would—which I basically am—I notice again his handsome features and his confident stride. I duck down into my seat as he walks past me in the parking lot. How is it possible that I am going in to meet that man? How is it possible that he is walking to meet *me*?

I check my lipstick in the rearview mirror. Why oh why couldn't he own a Honda Accord? Or a Toyota Camry? Even an Audi would be better than an Aston Martin! I thought the date had been going well, but he probably asked me to dinner only because he was hungry, not because we were "progressing." I check my wallet to make sure that I have enough money to pay for my half of the bill.

I walk into the restaurant feeling sweaty and scruffy. Why didn't I suggest a diner or maybe just feign illness and go home? I see Rick waiting by the hostess stand and marvel that he somehow looks appropriate wearing the same clothes that he wore to the zoo, while I feel like I need to go home, shower, and start all over again.

"Hi," he says. "I don't know how I beat you. I thought I saw your car in the parking lot."

I hope he didn't see me ducking underneath the window.

"It looks crowded," I say, changing the subject.

"She said it would only be a few minutes."

The sole bench is occupied by a quartet of twentysomething hipsters, so Rick and I stand in the busy waiting area until the hostess calls us. True to her word, our table is ready before I have a chance to get too anxious. She leads us to the far end of the sushi bar, and we sit at the only two vacant stools at the counter. Rick likes all of my favorites and orders them in Japanese. We share a large Kirin, and I notice that he doesn't drink too much of it or try to get me drunk. I am just starting to forget how sweaty and underdressed I feel when I catch sight of Janine. She and her date are being led to a table on the other side of the room.

"What's the matter?" Rick asks, and he turns his head to look.

"Don't," I hiss and turn back to the chef, who is sternly placing another plate of yellowtail in front of us. "I thought I saw someone I knew."

Rick looks at me curiously but doesn't ask any questions.

I'm surprised to see Janine, but I'm even more surprised to see her date. He looks an awful lot like Ahma's hairy-bear dude, Stephen. But that wouldn't be possible. Would it?

"Is everything okay?"

"Fine, fine." I take another sip of beer. "I just saw an old high school friend of mine. In fact, she was my best friend until about a week ago. We got into a horrible argument."

"What about?"

"About you. Not about you personally, but about you in the abstract. It was more about dating and men and . . . honestly, I can't even remember what it was about because it wasn't really about that. It was about how she feels about me."

"Let me guess—she's jealous because you have an easy time dating and she doesn't?"

"It's actually the opposite."

"Oh, come on."

The bill comes, and Rick hands the waitress a credit card. I offer to pay, but he shakes his head. "It was my idea." With that simple statement, he manages to deflate the act of paying of any sexist implications.

As we walk out the door, I glance in Janine's direction. She is giggling as her overly friendly date nuzzles her neck. I can see his face better from this angle. It's definitely Stephen.

We step outside into the warm summer night. It is close to nine o'clock, but it is still light out. I appreciate the wisdom of driving in two cars. We'll avoid the temptation—and potential regret—of a drunken scramble in the back seat.

"I had fun at the zoo and dinner," I say, but my mind is elsewhere. What are the odds that Janine and Ahma would date the same guy? Green Hills isn't that small.

"Me too."

I fumble for my keys and unlock the door, painfully aware of the lack of glamour in owning a Toyota Camry.

"Thanks again for dinner."

"My pleasure." And then he swoops in to kiss my cheek. A light little peck that could mean anything, even nothing.

CHAPTER TEN

I see the backpack on the floor, where I left it when I came home last night. I kept the notebook in the backpack all week with the intention of returning it to Alice. But I was called in to a series of emergency meetings on Tuesday, which drove me to meditate for a good half hour in the courtyard to cleanse my mind of negative energy. The meditation was too successful in clearing my mind, and I completely forgot about returning the notebook. On Thursday, when I finally stopped by her desk, Bertha told me that Alice had already left for the day. I am only delaying the unpleasant task of returning the notebook to Alice, trying to think of how best to do it without letting her down or telling her too much.

Victor is out with friends. The house is quiet. The weekends are the hardest. Two long, lonely days without the bustle of work to keep me occupied. Maybe that is why I can hear the voice of Alice's father calling to me so clearly. There is nothing else to muffle it, no other voices to keep me company. He makes me feel as though I am not so alone. He seems to be a kindred spirit who, like me, is deserving of contempt and compassion in equal measure.

As a teenager he may have been heedless, but as an adult he was probably dependable and somewhat dull. A dentist with a nice family. Responsible and restrained but with a passion that ran so deep it was indiscernible to others. I relate to his recklessness in falling in love with someone so different from himself, someone not entirely dissimilar from the woman I once loved. His story resonates with my own.

I recognize in him my own ability to keep secrets. Nobody ever suspects that people like us have secrets. But we all have secrets, things we keep from our families. Secrets we keep from ourselves. We soldier on despite our secrets, because that is our character and we do not know how to do anything differently.

I try to ignore his voice. Some secrets should remain hidden. Some secrets belong to the dead. But he has stories he wants to tell me. Stories that I should not hear but am helpless to resist.

~

February 9, 2010

The image I saw last night was of Shirley, as she was when we were in Korea. And what I experienced was not so much a dream as it was a vivid memory that I had not thought about in years.

She wore a plaid jumper with brass buttons on the shoulders. Her hair was in pigtails, a style that was much too young for her. We were sitting on the ground underneath the leaves of the Japanese maple tree. Its wide branches shielded us from view like protective arms. We alternated between the maple tree and the chestnut tree and the pine tree, trying to be careful not to meet in the same spot twice in a row. It was early autumn, and when the leaves drifted off the maple trees, they looked like baby hands waving. Unlike the pine tree when it dropped its cones, the maple leaves felt like gentle caresses on our heads. I sensed that Shirley was not in an affectionate mood, and though it was immensely difficult, I showed deference to her feelings. She sat cross-legged in that alarming way Americans have, with no apparent sense of modesty and no attempt to shield her underpants from my restless eyes, which could only peer at what my hands could not touch.

"Sit closer to me," she said.

I took her hand and cradled it between both of mine.

"You seem sad," I told her.

She started to cry quiet tears of resignation. I held her in my arms and told her that she could tell me anything. She shook her head, but eventually she told me that she would die if someone else did not share the pain of her secret. She told me the most horrible story then, about her father. How he came into her room at night, when her mother was asleep. How his hands aggrieved her body. Only his hands, she said, as though to defend him. Not anything else. He'd warned her never to tell anyone or he would send her away forever. He had been doing this since she was eight.

I stared in disbelief at her tearstained face as she spoke. She raised her eyes to meet mine. I didn't know what I could say. I knew there was nothing I could do to reassure her. What I wanted to tell her was childish and immature, "Let's run away!" But I was too sensible for that, too aware of the impracticality. We had no place to go and no money.

Instead, I pulled her closer, and clinging tightly to each other, we both cried.

For too long afterward, I could not look at Shirley without remembering what she had told me. It changed something between us, although I can't say what.

∿

February 12, 2010

These days, I am eager to fall asleep so I can be near her again. I am so eager that I no longer shower in the evenings but wait until the mornings. I bring the sweat and dirt from the day into bed with me. This repels my wife, who continues to bathe in the evenings. She massages cream into her face and lotion onto her legs. I notice only because she does this while I am trying to watch television. While she brushes her teeth, I turn off the television and pretend to be asleep. She slips into bed next to me as I lie perfectly still. I close my eyes and wait for Shirley. My wife lies awake and waits for me.

~

February 16, 2010

The memories appear more frequently. The burning smell of roasting chestnuts. Peeling away the hard shells, burning the tips of our fingers and our tongues as we popped them into our mouths still steaming. We huddled together with our bag between us in the courtyard. The other children played, running around in circles, kicking balls. Shirley and I were too old for games now, after everything that had happened between us. But we were not too old for hot chestnuts.

My wife brings me coffee every morning. She places it on the counter, beside the bathroom sink, while I shower. I can smell the rich aroma despite the perfume from my shampoo. The coffee is always strong and welcome, even if I resent my wife's intrusion while I shower. I breathe in the steam and close my eyes. I lather my scalp into white puffs. I rinse away the traces of Shirley's visit.

"Do you remember?" she asks. "Do you remember that time underneath the pine tree?"

Of course I remember.

"Do you remember what you told me?"

That I love you. That I will love you forever.

"Do you remember what happened then?"

A pine cone fell from the tree and hit me on top of the head. You said it was God punishing us.

"But you didn't agree," she said. "You said you didn't believe in God."

Yes.

"You said you only pretended so we could keep seeing each other."

Your parents—remember why you were there.

"In that godforsaken country."

Still littered with garbage from the war. You were like sunshine breaking through the smoke.

"There was no running water in your house," she says.

No toilets. No food.

"My parents were there to feed you and to save your soul. You and your parents and everyone else in the country."

In that they failed.

"Do you believe in God now?"

It was a pine cone. Falling from the sky.

"It left a bump on your head."

The bump never went away.

"Do you remember how you tried to crack the hard shell to get to the nut? You almost broke your tooth."

I can still feel the bump on my head.

"You could not get a single nut, even though we were hungry."

I'm sorry.

"You promised me that you could. You told me you would do anything for me. But you wouldn't even lose a tooth for me."

I loosened it. I cannot drink anything too hot or too cold even now, or it causes me pain. I cannot eat dried cuttlefish anymore. It used to be my favorite snack.

"That is nothing. That is nothing compared to what I had to do for you."

I'm sorry.

"That isn't enough."

It's all I can do.

"Is it?"

I write this down as quickly as I can remember it, afraid that the dream will disappear. I can still hear her voice whispering in my ear. I rub the top of my head, feeling the rise of my scalp at the crown. Is it my imagination, or does it feel tender this morning? I wiggle my loose tooth with my tongue. It is a miracle that I have been able to retain it for so many years.

~

February 18, 2010

At dinner, my wife confided that she thinks Alice is having marital problems.

"She hasn't called in several days," she said.

"Maybe she's busy."

"Alice is never busy. Perhaps we should invite them for dinner?"

The prospect does not fill me with joy the way that I imagine it should. My daughter is kind enough, but she has not fulfilled the potential she once had before she went to college. It would be easy to blame her husband. He is unambitious—or, rather, wrongly ambitious. He has delusions of being a great musician, but in fact he is mediocre. My daughter, with her years of piano lessons, must realize this, but if she does, she says nothing. He is kind, and I enjoy his company because he leaves me alone. He does not pester me with attempts to befriend me. He does not ask me bothersome questions about my dental practice, or my golf game. We can sit together on the couch while my daughter and my wife perform their ritual dance of intimacy and repulsion, each trying to impress and insult the other with subtle expressions and well-chosen remarks that strike to the core of who they are. They are as deft as geishas in their nuanced performance and just as irritating to watch. In fact, I must admit that I prefer the company of my son-in-law to my own daughter. *He is not my responsibility, and his shortcomings are not my fault. My daughter, on the other hand, is the product of all my efforts, my hopes and my dreams. She is the embodiment of the love I shared with my wife. Perhaps that is why she is a failure. When I see Alice, I see frustration, broken promises, missed opportunities. I see myself, unfinished and unfulfilled.*

~

February 20, 2010

The dinner with Alice and Louis was just as uneventful as I had imagined. Despite my wife's nosy questions, whispered loudly in Korean in the kitchen, Alice refused to open up. Or perhaps she had nothing to reveal.

"I told you things were fine," I told my wife after they had left.

"Things are not fine! Did you see how they sat?"

I could recall nothing strange in their postures.

"They did not touch each other once," she said.

"They never touch each other in our presence."

"Even when they were out of our sight, they did not. When they walked to the car, they did not hold hands as they used to. Alice did not lean her head toward his to whisper a belittling remark about us as they left."

"And that causes you concern? I would think that should please you. That was something you complained about so bitterly. Now you complain that it has stopped."

"It used to annoy me, certainly. But now it worries me. When she whispered to him, she was showing that she was closer to him than to us. What happens when intimacy disappears between a husband and wife?"

I refused to look at her. "Speaking of whispers, do you think Louis is stupid as a rock? When you whisper with Alice in the kitchen, do you think he doesn't suspect who you are talking about?"

"He couldn't understand me. I was speaking in Korean."

"Precisely why it is nonsensical to whisper! You may as well have been two schoolgirls passing notes in class! You could not have made it more obvious to our daughter's husband that you were speaking ill of him."

My wife paused for a moment.

"Alice says she is having financial problems," she said. "One of her clients has hired a full-time accountant. Louis is working less and less, and he spent twenty thousand dollars to make a CD. It was nearly all of their savings. He is getting older—too old to continue dreaming like this. He made a promise that this was his last shot. If he couldn't make it happen, then he would quit and find a real job."

"What kind of a job could someone like that get? He's never even had a real job."

"He's a smart man. He went to college. Got good grades, too."

"That was twenty years ago."

"He should find someplace that will provide them with benefits. They pay too much for their health insurance!"

I nodded. Everything my wife said was true. I should wish for more for my daughter, but the idea of my son-in-law working a nine-to-five job with benefits saddens me.

~

February 21, 2010

Shirley did not visit me last night. Instead, I dreamed of a woman wearing rags, her face obscured by a large gray hood. I approached, and she held out a hand to me, begging me for something. I dug in my pockets to give her some change, but I had none. She shook her hand impatiently while I frantically emptied all my pockets, my wallet. Finally, I handed her a credit card, which she started to eat.

"No! No!" I told her, but she would not relinquish it. I watched helplessly as she ate it all.

"I'm still hungry."

The voice was unmistakable. I pushed back the hood. But it was not my daughter. It was my wife.

It was no surprise that when I woke this morning, I was irritable and confused. My wife had left a cup of coffee, now lukewarm, by the bathroom sink. When I came into the kitchen, I saw that she had already made my toast and the one scrambled egg that my doctor permits.

"My coffee was cold."

"It wasn't when I brought it to you," she said with what she must have supposed was a beguiling smile. She was wearing an old dress that bunched in the front and clung to her many lumps and rolls. Where was the beautiful girl I had married? Time has slowly erased her looks, her figure. Sometimes I get a sense that this deterioration is for my benefit, that it is a form of revenge. Without her physical charms to distract me, I am forced to confront the essence of the woman I married, if I can find it. But I don't even bother to search.

"You were talking in your sleep," she said. I waited for her to continue, but she did not.

"What did I say?"

"You said, 'No!' You said it several times."

"Was that all?"

"Yes. But it wasn't just that. You were struggling, as though you were trying to fight someone off."

"I had a dream that Alice was a beggar woman."

"Our conversation must have upset you."

I sat down at the breakfast table and took a bite of toast. My wife puttered in the kitchen, rinsing glasses, organizing cutlery, with a determination that indicated that she was planning something.

"Was that the first time?"

"The first time what?" she asked.

"The first time that I spoke in my sleep."

"I can't remember."

When I returned from work, my wife had left newspaper clippings on the table instead of dinner. They were from the Korea Daily News. *I picked one up and read it. They were job listings.*

"What is this?"

"To help Alice. I went through the recycle bin and found all the old issues of the newspaper."

"Don't you think Alice is doing that already?"

"Not the Korean newspaper." Of course, she was right. Alice would not be reading the Korean paper. We had never bothered to teach her how to read hangul.

~

February 24, 2010

My wife is triumphant. Alice called eleven of the job listings that my wife had given her. Most were filled, but a library in the Restin area had a need for a part-time bookkeeper. Alice had an interview with the librarian, a Korean man, my age. I can't imagine any Korean man who would be a librarian.

My wife said that Alice thinks he looks like me but he doesn't act anything like me. I am glad to hear that. My wife looked at me so expectantly. Finally I said, "You are a good mother." She beamed. I knew I should say something more. "You have a lot of initiative," I added. This is true. In some ways, my wife is more American than my daughter. She works hard, and she is quite shrewd. I think that if she had not been beautiful, she would have been happier. The beautiful ones end up married, entrusting their futures to unworthy husbands—husbands who don't make enough money, husbands who don't love them enough. The homely ones—if they are hardworking and smart—end up like my cousin, Min Joo, who was successful, rich, and emotionally undemanding. As she grew up, her parents lamented Min Joo's big face, her tall, sturdy build, and her thick and shapeless daikon legs. My aunt blamed my uncle's blockheaded father, and my uncle blamed my aunt's athletic brothers. Neither wanted genetic credit for Min Joo. Nobody would marry such a girl! They feared they would be stuck with her forever. But Min Joo was smart, receiving higher marks in school than her two beautiful sisters and her handsome brother. Unlike her sisters, who dropped out of college after they received marriage proposals, Min Joo was forced to complete her education. She got a job in a seamstress shop, rising early and working late. She saved enough money so that within a couple of years, she could afford a ticket to the United States. Her parents were relieved. They didn't have to worry about some good-looking hustler taking advantage of Min Joo. They didn't even have to worry that she would get mugged, since she was as strong as any man, and she didn't have much money anyway. Within a few years, Min Joo had started a business importing into the US clothing manufactured in Korea. Imagine—my large and homely cousin, a fashion tycoon! The last I heard, she was living in a mansion in Beverly Hills, still childless but no longer alone. No, Min Joo had found herself a boy toy, a good-looking Italian model half her age! No worries about him trying to swindle her out of her hard-earned fortune—I hear that she gets a new boyfriend twice a year, like getting her teeth cleaned. Her beautiful sisters, on the other hand, have been married to the same men for over forty years. They live in the same houses they lived in when they first got married, in the same small village outside Seoul. Their husbands turned out to be less savvy than Min Joo, and so their wives work like peasants to make a living. Her handsome brother, still unmarried and chronically unemployed, lives with his parents.

Maybe if Alice had been born ugly, she would be happier. Instead, she has a pleasant smile, fair complexion, long legs, a trim figure. She is smart, but what has she done with her intelligence? She got married—and what does she have to show for that sacrifice? No children, no house, no money. At least they should have love, but I don't see it. In fact, I have never seen it. So why did she marry?

I don't worry that they are experiencing marital troubles, like my wife does. In fact, I would be pleased if that were the case. Maybe then, she would wake up out of her mediocrity. She might then be spared the kind of passionless life that so many of us end up leading.

~

I close the notebook. I was wrong. This man is not a kindred spirit. He is nothing like me. I would never speak so cruelly about my child. His harsh words would crush Alice if she read them.

This man has everything, and yet he is dissatisfied. His wife is loving. His daughter beautiful and kind. Yet, he has nothing but sour words to say about them. He cannot appreciate what is right in front of him. He is a fool. A fool with memories that refuse to be buried, that can do much damage to those he left behind.

I have a bad feeling, a premonition. It tells me that I should stop, that I should read no farther. But if I stopped reading now and returned the diary to Alice Markson, I would always wonder about the rest of the story. My mind has already started to imagine. It has the ability to concoct the most improbable scenarios. I would not be able to erase the questions that have arisen in my mind, that are becoming harder to ignore.

His voice beckons me. Although I want to put it away, I open the notebook and continue reading, if only to disprove my imagination, if only to prove myself wrong.

~

February 26, 2010

Shirley and I had made plans to meet again, in the woods, in three days' time. We always made sure to set an irregular schedule—different days, different times, and different meeting spots. Sometimes she was to arrive first, other times I was. We were never to be seen walking together. If we passed each other on the street, we ignored each other, although I couldn't help myself from looking at her out of the corners of my eyes.

It was late autumn, and the air was crisp that day. Orange maple leaves drifted down and landed in my hair. I crunched them underfoot as I paced anxiously. I glanced around, wondering whether Shirley had gotten lost or held up by her parents. I waited until the wind turned mean and chilly and the light had faded from the sky. I hurried home, already thinking of some lie to tell my mother for why I was late. I wondered whether I had gotten the date wrong, or the time. I hoped Shirley wouldn't be mad at me. I went back to the same place the next day, at the same time, thinking that maybe I had misremembered the day. But she did not show. I wandered by the missionary center where her parents were assigned. I was surprised to see new faces passing out tins of Spam and chocolate bars and cotton T-shirts. I learned that the Smiths had gone back to America so that their daughter would be properly educated. I wondered whether Shirley had known this when we last met. I wondered why they had left so suddenly. Shirley had become friendly with some of the local girls. Wouldn't her parents have given her a chance to say goodbye to them? Wouldn't they have wanted to let us know that they were leaving?

In the end, I guess we didn't warrant anything. They had done enough, they probably figured. The Lord's work was done. Perhaps they knew that many of our neighbors did not really believe in Christ. They took the free handouts but continued their ancestor worship on holidays, their visits to fortune-tellers and shamans. Maybe the Smiths were fed up with the deception, the hungry mouths, the grasping hands. Or maybe they were just tired of the lack of friends, and missed their home tongues and the smell and taste of familiar food and the sight of faces that looked like their own. Those are longings that I understand and for which I cannot fault them.

But even then, I knew what had really happened. Even though I invent other reasons, other explanations, I cannot alter the truth. Because what

Shirley told me during our last visit is something that I wish with all my heart had never happened, but it was the obvious consequence of our love. I can still see her eyes filling with tears as she searches my face, for . . . what?

"What would you do if I had a baby?"

My heart stops now as I remember, as it did then.

"Why?"

"Just what if? What if I got pregnant? It could happen, you know. Because of what we've been doing. It could happen."

She is watching me closely. I don't speak. I only stare back at her in terror. Then she smiles.

"I scared you, didn't I?"

I smile with relief. It was only a test.

"But what would you do?"

I shrug. I am only a boy, after all. Only fifteen years old. What can she expect from me? I reach for her and pull her to me. Her kiss is a little colder than before, her lips pressed hard against her teeth.

∼

March 1, 2010

Last night, Shirley returned to me. She caressed my cheek and my hair.

She placed a finger to my lips and whispered, "Sssshhhh." I woke with a start. My lips felt cold, and then the feeling spread to the rest of my body. My wife continued to sleep soundly beside me.

It was then that I realized the reason for Shirley's visits. She was dead, and she wanted me to join her.

SECRETS AND LIES

CHAPTER ELEVEN

My teacup is empty. The house is dark. I have been reading for longer than I intended. I hear my son's footsteps in the hallway.

"Appa?"

I start to hide the notebook and then remember that he cannot read hangul. For once, I am grateful for that. I am ashamed of what I have done, that I have read so much. This is not something that I should be reading. It is full of secrets. Secrets and lies.

"Why are you sitting in the dark?"

"Saving electricity. Fossil fuel. Greenhouse gases. Global warming."

He smiles. "Did you eat?"

"Not yet," I say. "And you?"

He lifts a paper bag into the air. "Macho's Tacos burritos. With hot carrots."

"And jalapeños?"

"Of course." He flips on the switch, and light fills the room. My son is wearing faded blue jeans and a well-worn T-shirt with a large blue square across one shoulder. The square means nothing; it's merely a design. My son tends to wear T-shirts with graphics that don't mean anything but look interesting. It's just one more thing about him I don't fully understand. His hair is ruffled from running around all day. If I didn't know any better, I would think he had spent all morning trying to look artfully disheveled. His skin is clear, as it has always been, even in adolescence. My son got only the best genes from his mother and me. He inherited his mother's smooth complexion, his height and strength from her side of the family, all large Midwesterners of Norwegian ancestry. Her family had some professional athletes in the bloodline somewhere, at least one football player and a distance runner. From me, he got the thick head of hair, so black that it sometimes looks blue. The straight white teeth, the high cheekbones—those are also my genetic contributions. Only his eyes reflect the combination of us. Dark as mine but wider, with her thick lashes. They are double folded, *sankapoohl*, but they are still Asian. Sometimes when I look at him, I can see his mother. Other times, it is my own gaze staring back at me.

He gets plates from the cupboard, even though he would do without them if he were alone.

"Traffic was terrible on the freeway."

"It always is."

"My arm still hurts from the shot."

He rubs his arm. His departure date hangs over my head like the sword of Damocles. I take a bite of the burrito. Victor is finished with his burrito before I am even done with my second bite.

"You must remember to swallow."

He laughs. "I'm storing it away, like a camel. No Macho's Tacos in Nicaragua."

"Yes, but surely tacos."

"Nobody makes them like Manny," he says.

"No, probably safe to say that's true."

"Too bad I can't bring along a secret stash."

"Wouldn't last the plane ride. Anyway, those tacos are a national treasure. Security wouldn't let them out of the country."

"It looks like I'm going to have to check luggage for the first time in my life."

"What, did they issue a ban on backpacks?"

"Naw, but I should bring a stash of toothpaste and sunscreen."

I wonder why he feels the need to save the world. His idealism is understandable, expected. I remember feeling the same way once, believing that I could change the world. But he has a restlessness that puzzles me. I wonder whether it is because his mother left us. But then again, I believe that everything is a consequence of her leaving. It's been more than six months since her death, and in my mind she is still the agitator.

"Your mother would worry about you being down there."

Victor gives me a sidelong glance, head tilted downward. "Yeah, maybe. But she's dead." His voice is gentle, a caress that he won't give me, constrained as we are by the boundaries of being male. He gathers up the remains of his dinner. He doesn't look at me. He still feels guilty although I'm not quite sure why. Maybe because he has recovered, at least by comparison. He throws his trash away and heads upstairs.

"I'm going out later tonight with some friends from law school."

"Another going-away party?"

He smiles. Victor has many friends who will miss him, but not as much as I will. He has been living with me since his law school graduation in late May. At first, it was awkward having someone else in the house. I had lived alone for so many years. Victor had moved out of the house when he went away to college. I think he wanted to escape the drama at home, his mother's constant disappearances and reappearances. She paid him too much attention, and me too little. She cherished him, but the way she treated me pained him. Victor is like that, empathetic and caring. I think he did not want to choose sides, although he couldn't help it. He has always been my ally. During the summers, he found jobs and rented an apartment instead of coming home. It was easier, he explained, he didn't need a car in Boston like he did in Orange County. It was easier for him to find work. He made enough during the summers to pay for a significant part of his tuition, cobbling together money from grants, loans, and other sources to make up the rest, asking me to cover only what he absolutely couldn't manage. I was proud of him, even though I missed him. And I was grateful that he didn't come home, especially the first couple of summers after Crystal River left me. She had gone before, but only for a night or a couple of days. But the last time she left, she took some of her things, and I knew she wouldn't be coming back. I needed time alone then, to fall apart. I could fake it at work, for a few hours. I could distract myself with meetings and personnel matters, order forms and reports. But by the end of the workday when I was home again, my heart grew heavy, my spirit diminished. I could no longer ignore the questions that repeated themselves in my brain. What should I do? What should I have done? Alone in my empty house, I opened a bottle of wine and drank. I fell asleep in front of the television. I slept in dirty sheets and left the curtains unopened. In the morning, I showered, dressed in clean clothes, shaved, and brushed my teeth. I was careful to present to the world an unfractured self. Was there anything more pathetic than an abandoned husband? I didn't need to inspire any more pity than I already received.

It was worse to work with women during that time. They sensed my hurt and gathered around me protectively, not saying anything but giving me searching looks to see whether I was okay, not suicidal or depressed, wanting to help somehow. Their pity made me feel even more pathetic. They tried to help by doing my work for me, not realizing that I welcomed the distraction. I occupied myself so that I wouldn't have to go to lunch with anyone and endure sympathetic, pitying, well-intentioned looks. Then I rushed home to escape the stifling atmosphere, only to remember that I had nothing to rush home to. The closer I got to home, the lighter my foot became on the pedal, until I was coasting the last block. I always sat in the car for a while, sometimes an hour, before getting out. Time was my enemy then. "Time heals all wounds," everyone said. But time was my tormentor. It created its own hell.

How did I recover?

I didn't. But I got tired of being sad and dirty and drunk. The whole ritual of mourning became tedious. I was bored out of my depression.

But recovery? I did not recover. When I think of what happened, my whole body turns gelatinous. The betrayal of abandonment turns my stomach like eating raw chicken. It clouds my mind like sleep. How could I have been so wrong? Did she deceive me, or did I deceive myself?

I think of Alice's father's notebook. I realize now what draws me to his voice. It is not because he reminds me of myself. It is because he reminds me of my ex-wife.

~

March 7, 2010

Sometimes when Shirley visits me, she comes in various disguises, yet I always know that it is her. Sometimes she has a parrot's face or roars like a lioness. Other times, she shines as though she were made of gold like a television angel. But I still know that underneath the disguise, it is her.

These visits have left me tired and distracted during the day. Today, I poked the lip of one of my longtime patients without even realizing it until I noticed the blood. She was furious and stormed out of my office with the napkin still clipped around her neck like a baby's bib. The patients in the waiting room were quite alarmed. I called my receptionist Rachel, even though her name is Rose. I caught her whispering to Maria, my hygienist, the two of them furtively casting concerned glances in my direction. Perhaps they suspect the onset of Alzheimer's. But what I have is the opposite, because it will not let me forget.

I know that Shirley's visit last night is the reason for my annoyance with my wife this evening. I realize that my wife is not to blame for my disinterest, but it doesn't make me ashamed or less annoyed. In fact, it only compounds my irritation toward her, which has become something resembling anger. Maybe even hate. I want to provoke her, but she remains calm. She doesn't even raise her voice at me, as though she knows that this is what I want. I am waiting for a justification, anything to exonerate my guilty thoughts. But she is patient and kind. Dinner is ready every night. She does not expect me to help her. The only sign that she harbors ill feelings toward me is in the cup of coffee that she handed me this morning. There were tiny bubbles on the surface of the black liquid. When I mentioned them to her, she feigned concern. "It must be the dishwashing detergent, darling. I will be certain to use less next time." But I knew it was not detergent. I watched her carefully, but my wife is as deceptive as a crocodile lying motionless on a riverbank. She looked back at me without blinking. I took a sip of coffee. When she smiled, I knew for certain that the bitterness that I tasted was not ground Colombian beans but the foamy saliva of a resentful Korean wife. It was my penance, what I deserved. I noisily slurped the rest of my coffee. Good to the last drop.

Tonight, I will make love to my wife with a ferocity that she will not expect. I know that when I close my eyes, she will disappear and it will be Shirley who lies beneath me. I will not open my eyes until the morning.

～

March 8, 2010

My coffee was without foam or bitterness this morning. My wife sang softly to herself in the kitchen, happy for the loving she received last night. Why can't I be satisfied with this? But I can't.

I felt the tightening in my chest again today. I was at the breakfast table. My wife looked at me. Her face was pale with fright. But then the feeling went away, and I pushed aside her concerns and went to work.

I felt tired all day, so I came home early. My wife was watching a show on television. It was a home-improvement show where strangers fix up each other's houses. She scribbled down notes on a pad of paper.

"What are you doing?"

"Nothing." She put down the pad of paper. I walked over and lifted it up. She had scribbled the words quartz counter *and* French vanilla paint.

"What's this?"

"Ideas. Audience can give suggestions on how to improve the house. My suggestions usually match the experts! My ideas could raise the value of the house by many thousands!"

I threw the pad of paper onto the table at an angle so that it skidded and fell to the floor.

"This is how you waste your day." I turned and went upstairs.

A few minutes later, I returned downstairs to get a glass of water, as I was feeling rather warm and my face was flushed. My wife was still sitting in front of the television, her hands on her knees, staring with sad resignation at the pad of paper that she had not yet retrieved. When she heard me walk into the kitchen, she looked up and her expression changed. She smiled and rose and rushed over to get the glass out of the cabinet for me, suppressing the melancholy that had marred her features only moments earlier.

She is a good woman, although not the one I would have chosen if I'd had a choice. She deserves to have a husband who loves her. It is this admission that makes me realize that I do, in fact, love my wife. Differently, of course, from the way I love Shirley. My love for my wife is a different beast altogether.

~

March 11, 2010

Last night, instead of Shirley, a large shaggy dog came to visit me. I recognized that it was the old dog that used to live down the street from me in Korea, the one with arthritic limbs. It was much larger in my dream, the size of two Saint Bernards. It gnawed on its arthritic legs to remove the pain inside, but that only increased the size of the wounds. My wife was patting the dog's head, even though she dislikes dogs, and I realized that I was the dog, licking my own blood, chewing my own flesh. And then, in the strange manner of dreams, I was the one patting the dog that my wife had become.

~

March 15, 2010

More than fifty years have passed. Half a century. So often during that time, I wondered about Shirley. What was she doing? Where was she? Was she happy? I wish I were magnanimous enough to say that I hoped she was, that I hoped her life was full and complete without me. In my better moments, I wished her the very best. But more often, I hoped that she was dissatisfied with her life and that she thought of me during important times, like when she gave birth to her child or married her husband. I wanted to be there with her, to be in her thoughts. I wanted the memory of me to infiltrate her happiest moments, her milestones. I also wanted the thought of me to comfort her if she felt alone or sad. I hoped that she conjured up my image then, the way I so often do hers.

~

March 20, 2010

Sometimes it is just her voice calling from the darkness.

"John. Wake up. When will you come to see me? When will we be together?"

I've thought of Shirley often over the years, but the pain of heartbreak dimmed over time, and the memories faded in their intensity. But in the past few weeks, the dreams have awakened constant memories that are much more powerful.

Shirley has become more real to me during my dreams. No longer is she a vision in white with a golden aura. No longer is she an assemblage of my best and worst fantasies, a blue-eyed dragon one night and a flame-colored butterfly the next. Sometimes she looks just the way she used to. Sometimes she has wrinkles and glasses and gray hair. Sometimes she looks the way she did when I saw her again, wearing high heels and cuff bracelets, her thick hair still long and wavy but now layered. Because, miraculously, I did get another chance.

I didn't expect to see her. It was New Year's Day of 1980, the start of a new decade. There were only a handful of nice Korean restaurants in Southern California at the time. The Korean community was very small, even in the Los Angeles area. I was there with my family. We used to make weekly pilgrimages into Koreatown to buy groceries—things we couldn't get in the local supermarket in Green Hills, like Chinese cabbage for kimchi and soybean paste for stews and soups. We had ordered chewy rice cakes and dumpling soup to welcome in the new year. My wife was fixing Alice's hair when I caught a glimpse of the back of a woman's head across the room. She was sitting with a man who was facing me. He was Korean and about my age. In fact, he looked rather like me. I excused myself and headed for the restroom. I took a path that would lead in an L shape, right past their table and then behind it. I was too nervous to get a good look at the woman as I walked past, but as I turned right, I glanced up and saw that she was looking right at me. Her mouth opened slightly, and for a moment, time froze.

It had been nearly twenty-five years. A lifetime, but no time at all.

The man must have said something to her, for she turned back to him and shook her head. I continued walking toward the restrooms and then pretended to use the pay phone. A minute or two later, she appeared. She stood in front of me with her arms crossed. It was difficult for me to look at her face, now that she was within touching distance. What if it wasn't her? What were the odds? But there was no mistaking the color of her eyes, the shape of her lips, even if she no longer wore a schoolgirl's uniform or her hair pulled back tightly in two tortoiseshell barrettes. She stood there patiently until I realized that I was still pressing the receiver against my ear.

"Are you waiting to use the phone?" I asked, thinking that I had been wrong—this wasn't Shirley at all, just a woman who wanted to use the pay phone.

"John?"

I nodded, even though that had never really been my name.

She didn't smile, and I couldn't move. She slipped something into my pants pocket.

"Please don't call me after six." She walked into the ladies' room. I pulled a matchbook out of my pocket. On the inside cover, she had written ten digits in blue ink. Her number had the same area code as mine.

~

There are some things that you don't want to know, that really shouldn't happen because they contradict expectation. A starving man should not refuse food. Cats should not chase dogs. A protagonist should not die. But these things happen sometimes, and when they do, we are never prepared. Sometimes this is our own fault. Because even when we see the warning signs, we ignore them. We forge ahead, despite the gnawing dread, not because we are brave or want to know the truth but because we want to prove our feelings wrong. We want to deny what we know in our hearts to be true. This is never a good idea. It is far better to run, to close our eyes, cover our ears, and flee.

The bad feeling returns. It tells me that I should put the notebook down or, better yet, burn it. But fool that I am, I don't listen. Instead, I pick it up and continue reading.

~

March 24, 2010

I did not dream last night. Nor the night before. I wonder whether Shirley has stolen away all my dreams. I wonder whether she is still angry, whether my memories of our time in LA have made her remember, too.

I called her as soon as I could after seeing her at the restaurant, as soon as I got into the office after the holiday. I remember the day so vividly, even though it was nearly thirty years ago. I sent my receptionist on an errand and left the hygienist with my patient while I dialed the numbers that were smudged on the matchbook cover that I clutched so tightly in my hand. The blood rushed through my ears, and I could barely hear anything, even when her voice answered with a wary, "Hello?"

I wondered whether I should be doing this.

"I can't believe it's you," I said at last.

There was silence, and I worried that she might hang up.

"Hello?"

She was crying. It was a sound that broke my heart.

"Where are you?" I said. "I'll meet you. Anywhere, just tell me where."

And so the decision had been made.

We agreed to meet in a hotel in Beverly Hills. I made reservations at a four-star hotel that I could scarcely afford, but I couldn't bear the thought of meeting her at a dingy motel or a family-friendly Holiday Inn. We couldn't take the chance that a nosy neighbor would notice my car parked in front of her house, and meeting at my house was out of the question.

I took the day off to see her. No explanations for my office staff. Canceled appointments. It was unusual for me. I was typically so responsible.

We agreed to arrive separately, as Mr. and Mrs. Chang. She liked this, the ability to change identities. She had taken her husband's last name and changed her first to one that recalled her favorite place in the mountains, with a rushing crystal-clear river. But she would always be Shirley to me.

I told her that a key would be waiting for her at the front desk if she arrived before I did. When I checked in, the clerk informed me that my wife was already in the room. My heart leaped at the idea—Shirley as my wife! I practically raced to the elevator. Shirley—waiting for me! I wanted to know everything about her, everything that had happened to her during the past twenty-five years. Did she have children? What were their names? Who were her friends? What happened to her after she left Korea? Was she happy? What kind of car did her husband drive? Did she think of me often?

Room 894. I knocked once. She opened the door. I had so many questions, but when I saw her, they all disappeared.

I wish I could say that it was awkward. That we stared at each other, speechless. That we tried to find words to bridge the divide that time had created. I wish there was something that could attest to my conflicted feelings. But I had no guilt, no hesitation. I was a married man with a daughter, yet I felt like a schoolboy.

She closed the door. It was as if this was something that I did every day. It was as if hours had passed and not years. Why did it feel so familiar? Not comfortable, but familiar. I was overwhelmed with passion, my heart and body bursting with desire. My body remembered, as did hers. We made love in the fluffy bed with the excess pillows and the soft sheets. Our souls were as intertwined as our limbs.

And so it began. The phone calls and the secret visits. We knew each other so well, yet we still knew nothing about each other. We kept from *each other the names of our spouses, where we lived, the day-to-day of our ordinary lives. It was as if we wanted to create our own world where it was just the two of us, the way it had been when we first knew each other. But of course, the joy and the pleasure and the happiness and the ecstasy were possible only through secrets and lies and deception and delusion.*

~

March 25, 2010

We maintained our secret life for four years, which were both blissful and tormented. Our love changed the nature of time itself. The moments we stole together were both eternal and fleeting. The days we spent apart were endless, yet the years flew by so quickly.

And then one stolen afternoon, Shirley greeted me with a look on her face that could only be described as beatific.

"I'm pregnant." She enveloped me in her arms. I knew that she didn't have any children. She had told me that she couldn't get pregnant, that she and her husband had tried for years without luck. She worried that the abortion that she'd had so many years before had scarred her and made it impossible for her to conceive. But she was wrong.

"Are you sure?"

"Three tests," she said with a laugh. "All positive. At my age! After all this time. It's a miracle." She threw back her head and whooped joyously.

I was alarmed. Why was she so happy?

"What are you going to do?" I asked. Surely she wasn't planning to have the baby?

She looked at me and then smiled slightly, as though she thought I was making an ill-timed attempt at humor.

"What do you mean?" she asked. "It's what I've always wanted."

"But what would you tell your husband?"

The smile disappeared, but she didn't say anything. She just stared at me, looking stunned.

"Don't you think he would suspect something?" I asked.

My question seemed to suck out her spirit. She continued staring at me as though I were a stranger. I should have kept my mouth shut.

"It could be his." She said this meanly, and my blood chilled as I looked at her luscious mouth flattened into a straight line.

"But it's not. You know it's not."

I hadn't yet realized what Shirley had been thinking—that we would be together at last, that I would leave my wife and daughter, and she would leave her husband. We could start over, a new life, a new family, the way it should have been from the start. That was a scenario that was so foreign to me, so impossible, that I hadn't conceived of it. I had a duty to my family, and it didn't matter what my heart wanted. Leaving them was something I could not do, just as I could not fly. What would happen to them if I abandoned them for this . . . Caucasian woman? Not only would I be ostracized from my community, but my wife would be as well. She would be disgraced. She might even commit suicide, as I had heard other abandoned women did. I harbored no ill will toward my wife. She had done nothing to deserve my disloyalty. And my daughter—my daughter's future would be destroyed. She would never marry. She would never have children. She would be scarred for life.

It hadn't yet occurred to me that my wife and daughter might be better off without me, or that my wife might meet somebody better for her than me, somebody who wasn't in love with someone else. I loved Shirley more than anything, but that was not enough. Love was not greater than obligation.

Yet why didn't I see my obligation to Shirley? That question pains my heart still. Why couldn't I see that she was counting on me—and that I couldn't disappoint her again? It was a miracle that Shirley had returned to my life. That she would conceive with me—a second time—so many years *later, when she couldn't conceive with her own husband . . . why couldn't I see that as fate, as destiny? As duty?*

"You think I should tell him the truth?" she asked.

"If you do, we will never see each other again."

My words, imprecisely spoken in a second language, were meant as a fearful prediction of the eventual cost of our actions. Her husband would never let us see each other again if he found out. But I should have known by the way her expression changed that she heard my words as a threat and not as they were intended. How could something as simple as the wrong choice of words, so easily correctable, so irretrievably alter the course of one's life?

Shirley's manner became cool then, and when I put my arms around her, she shrugged me off and told me that she wanted to be alone. When I tried to kiss her goodbye, she turned her head and would not look me in the eyes. I thought I understood why she was upset. After all, she had wanted a baby for so many years. But what could be done about it? She would come around, I thought. She would see that it would be crazy to have this baby. It would destroy our lives. She would see that ending her pregnancy was the best solution for both of us. That it was the only way.

It wasn't until I was on the freeway, my foot firmly pressed on the gas pedal, that I started to regret what I had said. Why couldn't she have this baby—our baby? Why couldn't we be together? I decided then that I would do whatever she wanted. I would do anything to be with her, damn the consequences!

Then why did I wait until the next day to call her? Perhaps I wanted the time to be with my family, one last time to eat a meal cooked by my wife, watch television with my daughter, as though nothing had changed. Or maybe I waited simply because I thought I had time.

I waited until the next morning, when I knew her husband had gone to work and she would be alone. The phone rang and rang as I cradled the receiver to my ear, but there was no answer. I knew exactly what I was going to say: "Let's have our baby. Let's live the rest of our lives together!"

I thought of those words all afternoon as I examined x-rays and prodded bleeding gums.

I called her number again from a pay phone before I got on the freeway. I called yet again from a phone booth outside a grocery store near my house. I didn't call my wife to ask whether I should bring home a carton of eggs or a gallon of milk. My loyalty was to Shirley! My heart beat only for her! Still, there was no answer.

Then, recklessly, I called her again, this time from home. Against our agreement, I called her in the evening, while my wife was watching television in the next room and my daughter was studying upstairs.

"Hello?"

So this is what he sounded like, the man who slept next to the mother of my future child. The man who might even make love to her that evening. I felt suddenly sick to my stomach.

"Hello?"

I hung up.

I called her every day for two weeks from the office, but there was no answer. Then in the evenings. Each time, it was her husband who answered. Why didn't Shirley answer? Why didn't she pick up the phone and let me explain? I had lost hold of my senses for just a moment! It was all a misunderstanding. I would spend the rest of my life making amends for my senselessness, if only she would give me a chance! Then one evening, I heard a recorded message that the number I had dialed was no longer in service.

And that is how I managed to lose the love of my life a second time.

CHAPTER TWELVE

My hands are trembling, and though I have only a few pages left to read, I must stop. I should have stopped as soon as I suspected. But I wanted to believe that I was wrong, despite the suspicion that planted its seed as soon as I started to read this cursed notebook. I should have known better. I should have lived with uncertainty rather than have my fears confirmed.

The mind stores fragments of days, moments lived and tucked away, images and impressions, and sometimes an occurrence—a coincidence, a chance encounter, a random request—draws them together into an epiphany. And then, there is no more hiding from the truth. There is no place left to hide.

Crystal River was beautiful when we met, but not more beautiful than my Korean-born girlfriend, who was still waiting for me in Hawaii. Was it because she was the first Caucasian woman to show a sexual interest in me? Was it my desire to fit into a society where I did not look like I belonged? Southern California was a different place back then.

We met in the library. This is remarkable, since I don't believe she has set foot in another library since that day. She had run in to make a phone call, and I was on the phone. There was only one working pay phone in the entire building. I was making arrangements to fly back home. I had just finished my studies at a small private college in Los Angeles. There was no reason for me to stay on the mainland. I would work for the public library system back home, marry Sunny, and raise full-blooded Korean American Hawaiian children, as my brothers had done, and as I was expected to do.

In the days before we fell out of love, Crystal River told me that she thought it was fate that we met. Why else would you be on that phone? But she knew that the phone in my apartment wasn't working, because I had already told her that. I had run out of money and couldn't pay the phone bill, so they disconnected the service. My mother had arranged to call me at the library at a designated time. I was twenty-six years old, and my mother was still taking care of me, making sure that I was safe, that I had enough money, so that I could return home to her. But neither my mother nor I expected Crystal River.

She was standing in a sundress that came to well above her knees. She was wearing strappy sandals and a bracelet around her ankle. She wore lots of silver bangles and several necklaces with crystal pendants. She sparkled and jangled and tapped her foot impatiently, and when I looked up apologetically, she smiled. She opened her lips and bared her teeth, and I understood then that her impatience was not so that she could use the phone. She was waiting for me.

Crystal River told me that she forgot who she needed to call when she saw me.

"I didn't know you were Korean at first," she said later. "Your clothes looked too American—I thought you were probably Japanese. But when you looked at me, I could tell. By the expression on your face."

It was a queer thing to say. But I didn't think to ask her anything more about it. Everything she said was puzzling. She was living at Venice Beach, *on* the beach, in a sleeping bag. There were others like her who slept on beaches, who talked about freedom. It was 1969, and all the rules were breaking. She said she loved to see the stars at night. I had never even noticed the stars. The beaches in California were so different from what I was used to at home. They didn't seem much like beaches at all. They were strangely devoid of vegetation, crowded and noisy. The water wasn't blue but a grayish-green, like the sky.

I found out later that while Crystal River may have loved the stars, the main reason she slept on the beach was that she had run out of money. She had traveled from Sand Point, Idaho, to Boulder, Colorado, to Taos, New Mexico, to Los Angeles. I heard a complicated story of a man and then another man, but I didn't get into details. I had enough sense even then to know that it wasn't about a man but her need to move around, to see new things and experience life. As a child, her parents had moved around a lot. They were educated, devoutly religious, true believers. They dragged their only daughter around the world and back again. She told me that she had always longed for a place to call home, a big house with a wraparound porch, friends with whom she could celebrate more than one birthday. But as soon as she became old enough to break from her parents, Crystal River hit the road. It was what she had grown used to. "The world is my home," she said, her blue eyes twinkling and her dimples deepening, pulling me toward her like Earth's very core.

Crystal River was complex and exotic, which is what she thought of me. But she was wrong. I was simple in desires and plain in upbringing. I had come from a family of farmers, barefoot for most of my childhood, cocooned by lush vegetation and temperate weather. Where I came from, I was ordinary. The most remarkable thing about me was that I managed to complete my degree on the mainland. Ironically, that was the thing that Crystal River found most plain. She wanted me to teach martial arts, do yoga, carve wood, sculpt pots—make something with my hands, with my body—but I stubbornly refused. It was the only way that I could resist dissolving, the only way I could cling to the scrap that was left of who I was. She could bend and twist reality out of shape with her strange brand of illogic. But my Confucian beliefs were deeply embedded into my cells, and even Crystal River couldn't change the one thing that I knew for sure—that knowledge reigned supreme over impulse and feeling, that the brain ruled the body. Except when it came to her. We married that summer, before I even told my parents that she existed.

She told me that she had grown up with parents who were faithful believers in Christ, in spirits, in hell and heaven. She smiled wryly when she said this, and her nose crinkled as though she had smelled something foul. She didn't like to talk about her parents, and she hinted that bad things had happened to her that had made her lose faith in religion. What she believed in most was what she could touch, what she could feel. With her hands and with her heart. And when she no longer felt me in her heart, she found another body to touch.

She was as improbable as her name, and she corrected anyone who tried to call her Crys or Crystal. "A crystal river is a different thing altogether," she'd insist. Of course, Crystal River wasn't her true name. Like much else about her, it was constructed, her attempt to control her destiny. An irony, given her belief in fate, in the inability to control her passions. Everything was the result of the planets and the stars aligning a certain way, she proclaimed, exerting a gravitational pull on all living creatures, who were full of magnetic energy. Crystal River was full of that sort of baloney. Yet I loved her for all of that, her illogic, her contradictions, her beauty. I loved the way her ankles curved into her feet, and the way she set her mouth so firmly when she was angry. I loved her for the history that we shared and the son that we made and the drama that she imbued into my life. My life had been nice before then. My path was clear. She promised to make the journey much more exciting. I didn't know then that she would not accompany me to the end.

I was drawn to her vitality. She had so much passion for life when we first met. That was what I missed the most as time passed. She seemed to grow quieter, smaller, shrinking with each passing day. She seemed to disappear, even before she left.

Were there warning signs? That is the question everyone wants to ask but doesn't dare. Because of course, there always are. The phone calls and the hang-ups. The unexplained crying jags. I assumed she was depressed and suggested that she see a psychiatrist since analysis was much in vogue at the time. She refused, saying it would do no good, and I didn't push the matter. Then, much later, there were the absences, the drinking, the pills that appeared in prescription bottles that she stashed in the refrigerator and underneath the sofa cushions. She forgot things—dinner dates, birthdays, anniversaries, her car keys. She didn't remember the nightmares that made her cry out in her sleep, that made her angry and weepy the next morning. But what was there to do about any of it? What is there ever to do? In the end, there is nothing to do but prepare, which is why it is so much easier to cling to the belief that things will return to the way they used to be and to transform the mythological past into some magical future reality. But like a mirage, that future, just as we draw near, disappears.

Crystal River had lived in Hawaii when she was a teenager. She loved the way the breeze felt on her skin and the smell of flowers and the sea. She imagined that, marrying me, we would live in a *hale* on the beach, forever barefoot and sun-tanned and untroubled by reality. Against my better judgment, I took her home with me, to my family, as my wife. Perhaps it was because I had married her without obtaining my parents' approval. Perhaps it was because she was white. Perhaps it was because Sunny, my old girlfriend, was like a member of the family. Or maybe it was something else. Maybe it was simply because my mother sensed, the way that mothers do, that Crystal River would never make me a suitable wife. Maybe she could tell, by the way Crystal River wore her hair loose around her shoulders, the way she walked, with hips that swung, the way she laughed, with her mouth wide open as though she wanted to swallow the world whole. Maybe it was her name, which was meant to conjure the natural world but was entirely fabricated. My mother knew that she would never be happy on an island, that she would always be gazing out at the wide expanse of blue sea.

Our first visit to my family was also our last. There was drama, yes. Things I don't wish to remember. Accusations, compromising situations, a gaze held too long with a distant cousin, an embrace interrupted. Voices were raised. Someone threw a glass. Crystal River shook it all off, and I refused to see, faulting others for the commotion she caused. My mother begged me to leave her, warned me that she was trouble, cried because I had disappointed her. My father threatened to disown me, told me that I would be sorry, that I was ruining my life, that I would regret this moment. I didn't care. For the first time in my life, I was rude and reckless and bold. For the first time, I was actually alive, or so Crystal River told me, and I believed her. How could I not believe her when her cheeks were flushed with life, her eyes so bright? How could I not believe her when she loved me so much, and I loved her more than I had ever thought I could love anything or anyone?

So we fled. We left Maui for Kona, where we enjoyed a real honeymoon. Although I had lived most of my life in Hawaii, I had never visited Kona, which is so different from where I grew up. Black ridges curved in circles the way water marks the sand on a beach, the result of heat melting the earth and marking it in patterns like waves, leaving it blackened and hardened. Crystal River and I swam in the warm waters with the sea turtles and the colorful fish. She was fascinated by the black lava rocks that jutted from the ground, rough as sandpaper. She picked one up that was the size of a pineapple.

"I want to take this back with us."

"It won't fit in our luggage."

"I'll carry it on in my bag."

"It's bad luck."

This interested her.

"How?"

"Legend has it that bad luck will follow anyone who takes lava off the island."

Crystal River smiled and shrugged her shoulders mischievously. She was fascinated by folklore and magic. When I told her that the royal family often wed brothers and sisters, believing that doing so would produce genetically superior offspring, her eyes widened with interest, and she tilted her head forward. Crystal River picked and chose her beliefs, unlike the locals, who had no choice but to believe. Against my better judgment, I let her take the rock, ashamed that I still felt the pull of such primitive superstitions. At night we made love as we listened to the rush of wind, the tropical breeze that sounded just like falling rain.

We returned to California, eventually settling in Orange County. Crystal River used the lava rock to decorate our front stoop. I left it there even after she moved out, hoping that she might return and that she would notice if it were missing. When she died, I placed it underneath the bed in Victor's room. I couldn't bring myself to throw it away, for it was still a memory that had significance. Anyway, doing so would not undo the bad luck that I was sure it had brought into our household. For I was still a Hawaiian boy inside, despite my leather shoes and my many years on the mainland, and I often wondered whether the problems that befell us were the result of this black rock. I remember once mentioning that to Crystal River, and suggesting that we return to Kona to take back the rock. But she merely laughed and said something about life's rhythms and the ebb and flow of good and bad experiences. So the rock stayed, even longer than the woman who'd brought it.

Were there warning signs? Yes, of course there were warning signs. A decent woman does not approach a stranger the way she approached me the first time we met, as though we already knew each other. She was so open and vulnerable that for the first time, I felt I could be strong. She made me want to rescue her from whatever she was fleeing from. She made me think that I—the boring son, the one who never made my mother worry—could be a hero, her courageous knight in shining armor. But in the end, I could not save her from her demons. I could only lose myself.

She told me very little about her family or her itinerant childhood, but not because she was trying to hide anything.

She told me she had been pregnant before, when she was a teenager, only fifteen, but she gave me few details, and I didn't pry. I had assumed it was when she was in Hawaii, where her family had lived when she was a teenager. When her parents insisted that she tell them who the father was, she refused.

"But I did tell them one thing," she said. "That he was Asian." She had believed that her parents, devout Christians, would have no alternative but to let her have the baby. But they didn't want a half-Asian grandkid. They packed their bags that very day and left on the first flight to New York City, where her condition was cured by a visit to an unmarked office down a narrow alley. The doctor had dirty fingernails and wore a surgical mask over his mouth at all times. Her parents waited in the car at the curb, as though making sure she would not escape.

"They didn't get out to help me into the car when it was over. They didn't say a word to me during the ride home or for a long time afterward."

She smiled sadly, and my heart swelled.

She left out the details—that she had been living in Korea, not Hawaii, that her parents had been missionaries and not simply religious fanatics—not to conceal the truth, but because it was too painful to remember. She simply wanted to forget, to escape the damage that had been done to her. She thought she could run away and reinvent herself, spin a life that was free from her troubled childhood. I understood this and did not pry or press for the specifics. They didn't matter, we told ourselves. What mattered was the present and that we were together. She did not intend to deceive me, not then, not yet. But in the end, we were unable to escape from her past.

I've often wondered whether it was me that she truly loved, or whether I was just a substitute for the one that she couldn't have. I tried to convince myself that what happened before we met didn't matter. I loved her—I love her still—and I loved the girl she was before we met, when she was a scared fifteen-year-old named Shulamite Smith.

She had told me her real name so long ago that I had nearly forgotten it. Her religious parents had named her after a biblical figure, a woman who inspired great passion in King Solomon. Shulamite might mean "peace" in Hebrew, but it would also mean being teased and bullied on the playground. She would have adopted a nickname, one that allowed her to fit in with her schoolmates. Instead of Shulamite, she would have gone by something more familiar. Like Shirley. She never told me about her nickname because by the time I met her, she had discarded it in favor of a new name, one of her own creation—Crystal River, after her favorite place in the mountains.

Of course, she did keep secrets from me, even if her name was not one of them. After so many years of trying without luck, why didn't I suspect that the child she carried wasn't mine? For we were never meant to be, Crystal River and me. Our DNA did not combine to form the perfect child, a child she delivered into my eagerly waiting arms. Yet, I cared for him as though he were mine, because I wanted to believe it. I could see in his face my features. I understand now it is only because her beloved looked like me—or, rather, that I looked like him. The realization pains me more than anything I have ever felt before.

She became increasingly erratic as the years passed. Now I wonder if it was because Victor's resemblance to his biological father grew as he got older. Did they look and act alike? Did their similarities increase with time? Did Victor develop the same voice, the same mannerisms and expressions? When Crystal River looked at our son, did she remember her betrayal of me—or her passion for her ex-lover? Was she tormented by guilt or by longing?

I knew she had affairs, but I ignored them. She was restless, seeking something that I could not explain. Even if she didn't come home at night, she eventually returned to care for her only child. But children grow up and leave, and then it was just the two of us. Her mood changed considerably when Victor left for college and worsened in the years that followed. She sat on the couch all day and watched television. She disappeared mysteriously for hours, even days, at a time.

Then, one day, she was gone for good. I didn't call the police. I wasn't worried by her absence in that way. I was saddened, but not worried. She called me two weeks after she'd left. She had moved into an apartment in Los Angeles, but she wouldn't say where, declining even to give me her phone number. We continued to share our joint bank account. I continued to pay her credit card bill. We never divorced. When she was found dead in her apartment, the police called me first because I was still her husband and she was still my wife. I will never forget the day I received the call: January 10, 2010. They said she had probably been dead two days.

A thought occurs to me. I turn to the first page of the notebook. The date is clearly marked in the upper-right-hand corner. January 8, 2010. The first person my wife wanted to see in the afterlife was not me or her son. It was her ex-lover.

∼

March 27, 2010

She is much more vivid now, more so than ever. She looms before me, as bright as the sun, as luminous as the moon.

137

"Why don't you join me?"

If only I could . . .

"It's time."

But how?

Shirley smiles. She beckons me to her. I reach my arms out to her, but it is not Shirley that I feel. It is my wife. I apologize, tell her that it was only a dream. She murmurs understandingly and goes back to sleep.

~

March 30, 2010

My heart is much lighter today than it has been for the past few days. Shirley's visit felt so real last night—more than ever before. Instead of floating above me, or in front of me, she was sitting on the edge of my bed! She was beautiful. Her blonde hair was silvery gray, and she was smiling. I sat up and looked at her—I couldn't take my eyes off her! She just sat there and smiled. She did not speak this time. I reached my hand out to touch her, to feel her in my arms, but as I did so, my wife stirred. I looked over at her in alarm, and when I looked back, Shirley had disappeared.

Was she angry? Was she jealous?

Perhaps I should feel concerned, but I cannot. The way she was looking at me—with so much love!

~

March 31, 2010

A very disturbing thing happened to me this afternoon. I was coming back from lunch when I felt a tightening in my chest, as though a noose had been fastened around my ribs and my back. It lasted about two minutes, and then it stopped. I became very dizzy and had to sit down. I was so shaken that I had to cancel the rest of my appointments for the day. A longtime customer, Mr. Renton, was very upset. I will have to offer him a free cleaning, and do it myself.

~

April 2, 2010

The last time I saw Shirley in Korea, we were sitting in our favorite place, underneath the chestnut tree. The dirt was softer there, for some reason. No grass grew at the base of the tree, perhaps because of the shade. The leaves and the chestnuts were starting to drop from the branches, but we were safe as long as we stayed close to the trunk. The tree grew on the slope of a mountain, far enough away from where my friends usually played in the field below. We heard a chestnut fall with a thud, and Shirley shook her head, still amazed at their size. She explained to me that in America, the chestnuts were much smaller, the size of walnuts. The tree we sat under had chestnuts much bigger. I felt proud when she said that, as though Korea's larger chestnuts could somehow remove the sting of having to receive food supplies and armed protection from the Americans.

"Chestnuts are kind of like coconuts," she said. Shirley had seen coconuts in Hawaii, where she had lived before coming to Korea.

"How so?"

"They don't taste the same, but they are both so difficult to open. What made the first person think there would be something worth eating inside?" She pointed to a rock nearby. "How do we know that there isn't some lovely-tasting juice in there? Or some delicious nut meat?"

I laughed, but not because I found her observation so humorous. We had been talking about other things, things that made me uncomfortable, and I was glad to have the conversation shift to Hawaiian coconuts. She, however, did not even smile. I kissed her on the lips, an invitation. But she turned away.

"I have to go home."

"It's getting late," I agreed. The sun was setting, and I imagined my mother was already calling me to come to dinner.

Shirley sat up and looked me in the eyes. "Home is where the heart is," she said, very seriously.

"Then we don't need to go anywhere."

She smiled a little then and returned my kiss.

~

April 4, 2010

A wise man said there is never any time for regrets. But I am not a wise man. I am a fool. Twice, I have had happiness within my sights, in my arms, and twice, I've let it go. Is it luck that gave me that opportunity when so many others never experience it? Or is it a curse to have felt something and to spend the rest of my life pining for that feeling?

If I hadn't truly believed that I could be happy with my wife, I would never have married. I would have stayed a bachelor for the rest of my days. When I met Young Ha, I was nearly over Shirley, or so I thought. She was a memory that I guarded within the deepest chamber of my heart. Young Ha was kindhearted, beautiful, and full of positive energy. My parents agreed that she would make a good wife. Certainly, they were relieved that I'd fallen in love at all, knowing how despondent I'd become after my American friend had moved away. If they only knew that what I felt was not the product of some silly unrequited crush! But they never even suspected—they could never imagine that Shirley, white as milk and seemingly as pure, would have such untamed impulses. They never could have dreamed that the feelings I had for her were as complicated and genuine as any love celebrated through marriage. My love for Shirley was stronger than what I felt for Young Ha as she stood in her Western-style bridal gown, complicated silk and lace and tulle veiling her face, trembling as she stood beside me and looking so serious, as though she were taking an oath of military service instead of reciting her marital vows.

I did love my wife. I must believe this. For if I did not, then why didn't I stay with Shirley when we had our second chance? Why didn't I acknowledge my life for the sham that it was and try to be honest about what I truly desired? It is a failing so profound that I can scarcely stand to look at myself in the mirror. What I see staring back at me with empty eyes is a haunted man, someone without a soul or a heart because he lost it so many years ago.

So why didn't I leave? I could claim it was duty to my family. That would indicate some measure of honor, of character. But I know that it was not out of obligation that I stayed.

So why did I stay? Because I was stupid, and too slow. Because I spoke words that I did not mean, and I waited to take them back. There would be no taking them back. I had waited too long.

I wonder what happened to Shirley. Did she confess our affair to her husband? Did she move on and forget about me?

Most of all, I wonder, Did she have our child?

CHAPTER THIRTEEN

I was hoping that I would have a chance to talk to Mr. Park and that he could give me an update on the notebook. He's had it nearly two weeks, and I'm starting to wonder if he's just forgotten about it. But on Tuesday, Bertha tells me he's out sick, and on Thursday, he's still not back. Bertha says that it's odd, because Mr. Park never gets sick. She can't remember him being absent for more than a day or two in the ten years that she's worked with him.

Rick and I have made plans to see each other again. A real old-fashioned dinner date. I text him directions to my house, and we decide that he will pick me up on Friday at six o'clock.

On Friday, I get stuck in late-afternoon traffic, so by the time I get home, it's nearly five thirty. I rush into the house and notice Ahma's purse at the bottom of the steps. She's usually not home before six. I call to her, and she answers from her bedroom. I climb upstairs to let her know my plans for the evening and see that she herself is getting ready for a big night on the town. She is wearing designer jeans with stiletto heels, burgundy lipstick, and black eyeliner, and her hair is blown out and sprayed stiff. It is terrifying to see my mother look so vixenish.

"A date?" I say.

She nods.

"Who is he?"

"Nobody you know."

"How did you meet him?"

"Regular way."

"What's that?"

"Way people meet. Someone at work."

"What's his name?"

She pauses, and then she says, "Harold."

"Harold what?"

She shrugs. "Don't remember." She brushes bronzer onto her temples and her cheekbones. "Saleslady said do this, looks healthy."

"You have on a lot of makeup."

"You like? Went to department store today. You can have it." She gestures to a small makeup bag with sample-size lipstick and skincare products inside. Her free gift with the purchase of seventy-five dollars or more.

"What does he do?"

"Businessman."

"What kind of business?"

"Development. Condos."

"That makes sense."

"What about you?" she asks.

"I have a date, too."

My mother looks as though I have sprouted wings and turned into the tooth fairy. "You?"

"Can you believe it? Even me."

"Not that way." She gestures to my outfit.

"I'm going to get dressed," I say. "What time is your date supposed to be here?"

"Six o'clock."

She applies one more coat of lipstick and mashes her lips together. She walks over to the bed and sits down.

"Mine, too." I glance at the clock. Only thirty minutes before our dates arrive.

I jump in the shower and shampoo and condition my hair. When I get out, I wrap it in a fluffy white towel while I throw on some jeans and a drapey gauzy blouse. I hope we don't go somewhere too nice. I let loose my hair, which immediately soaks the back of my blouse. I quickly blot it somewhat dry and do my best to slick back stray hairs with pink gel that I find at the back of the bathroom cabinet behind all the blow-drying accoutrements that I compulsively buy but never use. I apply some mascara, a little lip gloss, and a touch of eyeliner. I step back. Not bad. Not as hip and sexy as Ahma—my jeans are Levi's and I am wearing flat sandals—but okay. The doorbell rings. I glance at the clock. It's six o'clock on the dot. I search for my heels. The doorbell rings again. I'll have to answer the door. Ahma is practicing her "let man wait" routine. I run downstairs in bare feet and open the door.

The man standing before me is tall and thin with a disproportionately large, bald cranium and a broad, suspiciously ruddy forehead. He smiles, showing all his top teeth, the pointy canines touching his bottom lip like vampire fangs. He looks vaguely familiar, although I am certain we have never met.

"Lotus Flower?" he asks, raising his eyebrows.

"What?"

My mother tromps down the stairs, calling out irritably, "It's for me."

The man looks momentarily confused, but after he gets a good eyeful of my mom in her skintight jeans and heels, his smile spreads so widely that his gums are overexposed.

My mother grabs her purse and scowls at me. "Your date is late," she hisses and then shuts the door quickly behind them. I peer out the peephole. Her date is not entirely bald. He has a few straggly clumps of hair at the base of his neck. It strikes me why he looks familiar. He looks like the marabou stork that I saw at the zoo on my date with Rick.

Rick is late, but only by fifteen minutes. This gives me enough time to put on my shoes, reapply lipstick, and comb my hair properly. I'm still a bit miffed that Ahma's date mistook me for her—sure, she looks good for her age, but she is nearly twenty-five years older than I am. I open the door. Rick is holding a bunch of assorted flowers. He is wearing a smile, khaki slacks, and the perfect casual blazer.

"Hi," he says.

"Hi." I'm not sure that the flowers are for me—although I can't think of who else they would be for—until he practically shoves them into my arms. I rush around the house looking for a vase while Rick waits for me in the entryway.

"You live here with your mom?"

"Yes," I call from the kitchen. I am searching for a vase in the cabinet underneath the sink, but all I find are extra jugs of dishwashing detergent, rubber gloves, and bleach.

"Did you grow up in this house?"

"Yeah, pretty much."

"Nice home."

"Thanks."

"Cozy."

"Yeah." I don't find my house particularly cozy. It's a standard suburban tract home. The layout of this house is just like all the others on the block.

"Nice cul-de-sac," he adds.

"Yeah." I give up trying to find a vase and dump the flowers in an empty soup pot that I fill with water. I grab my purse and join Rick.

"Okay," I say brightly. "Let's go."

I shouldn't have been surprised when Rick pulls into the parking lot of La Chemise. Although Newport Beach is one of the most expensive places to live in the United States, the fine-dining options are somewhat limited. I glance around the large dining room, feeling woefully underdressed. I wonder if Ahma will show up with the marabou stork.

"You don't like this place," Rick says as the waiter seats us at a corner booth with plush orange leather seats.

"No, it's fine. It's very nice," I say. "I'm just wondering if I'll see my mom here."

Rick smiles good-naturedly. "Too stuffy?"

"Oh no, I didn't mean that at all," I say. I tell him about the marabou stork and then mention Ahma's outfit and her new makeup.

"She sounds like a blast," he says.

I glare at him. "She's my mom."

"You do want her to have a life," he says.

"Of course. Just not this kind of life."

"What do you mean?"

He is looking at me so earnestly, but I can't begin to tell him. How can I explain what I mean? That I don't want my mom to have to wear uncomfortable shoes at her age? That I don't want her to be vulnerable to the compliments of a department store saleswoman? That I don't want her to kiss men who look like vultures or call her Lotus Flower?

"Nothing . . . I guess it's just strange, that's all."

"It'll probably take getting used to. It's hard to see your parents date again, from what I understand. Fortunately, there were no kids involved in my divorce."

The question looms over our table like a storm cloud heavy with rain, but I don't dare ask him, and he doesn't offer. Maybe he thinks I don't want to have kids. Maybe he's afraid that I do.

The dinner at La Chemise is about what I expected, small portions covered in bland creamy sauces that somehow manage to be both filling and unsatisfying. Rick has ordered a bottle of wine, and that, on the other hand, is delicious. I make a deliberate effort not to fill the gaps in our conversation with nervous chatter, and every time the urge strikes, I take a sip of wine instead. Rick seems as comfortable with intervals of silence as he does with everything else.

He insists on picking up the tab again, and I don't argue, since I know that paying such a hefty bill would make me so resentful that it would undo any goodwill earned in paying it.

"It's really great to see you again," he says once we are alone in his car. I have never been in a nicer car. The leather seats are so soft and smooth that I have to restrain myself from rubbing against them. The control panel looks like that of a space shuttle, with digital displays controlling everything from the temperature to the music that we are listening to.

"It's great to see you, too," I say. My response sounds canned and tinny. My blouse suddenly feels too constricting, and I have the urge to open the windows but can't figure out which button to push. He is saying something about seeing each other again when he gets back from his business trip, and I turn and look at him and then, somehow, I am kissing him, full on the mouth. The feeling of his lips against mine, being so close to another person, is incredible. It's been a long time.

"Do you want me to take you home?" he whispers as he kisses my ear.

"To your home."

Traffic is light, and the drive takes only a few minutes on the freeway, and then up a winding road lined with flowering trees. His house is modern and beautiful, all lines and edges, with floor-to-ceiling windows that show off an amazing view of the ocean. A house in a magazine, and there he is, a man from a magazine, offering me a drink, which I decline. I don't want to have any regrets. We sit on his tasteful leather couch, and when he turns to me, I don't know why I feel so comfortable moving toward him, but I do. I reach under his shirt, and the physical chemistry is so strong that I understand now what it means to find someone irresistible.

We move to the bedroom, and I'm relieved that there is no awkward moment where I have to remind him to use protection. He knows what to do, and he knows his way around a woman's body, and I wonder if this is how it is supposed to be. Louis is my only other point of reference. Is this what I've been missing all these years?

When I wake up, it is early morning, and his arms are still wrapped around me. I turn toward him and think, *This is so perfect*. So perfect that there is no way it can last.

~

It is before six in the morning when I try to sneak into the house, but Ahma is already awake and emptying out the dishwasher.

"I guess a good date," she remarks.

I remind myself that I am a thirty-nine-year-old woman. I tell myself this a couple more times before I muster enough courage to ask, "How was your date?"

Her lips harden into a line, and her eyes turn down like a frown. "Nothing. Big zero." She turns back to putting the dishes into the cabinet.

I am halfway up the stairs when I muster up the courage to ask, "Ahma?"

"What?"

"Why did that guy think I was you?"

"What?"

"Why did he call me Lotus Flower?"

My mom is silent for a long moment, and I walk back down the stairs so that I can see her expression when she answers.

"Ahma?"

"How do I know?" she asks irritably. She slams the dishwasher shut.

~

Rick texts me later that day. Even though it's Saturday, we both know without discussing it that we won't see each other tonight. It would mean too much to see each other two nights in a row. It would create too much pressure.

That night, I dream that I am slowly walking down a dirt road alone. A vulture with a bleeding forehead is chasing me and I am trying to get away from it, but I am not walking quickly. I'm frightened, I can feel my heart racing, but I continue to walk at the same pace, simply because I am unable to move any faster. I feel the shadow of the vulture's wings over me, and the brush of its feathers, when mercifully I awaken. Although it's not hard to figure out where that nightmare came from, it troubles me so much that I am unable to get back to sleep. Finally, at five in the morning, I give up and log onto the computer.

I stare at the Yahoo! home page for a long moment, wondering whether I am still asleep and that what I see before me is just a continuation of my nightmare. Instead of the advertisements for low-rate mortgages and secret health remedies that typically populate the right side of the page, I am looking at my own grinning digital image. My setmeup profile with the words Lonely? So is she is being used as an *advertisement* on the Yahoo! home page! There, for all the world to see, is my height, weight, and best-case scenario for a date: sushi and a movie. But that's not the worst part. I realize to my horror that below the first ad is another one, with another setmeup profile and another caption—. . . or maybe you prefer . . .—followed by the digital image of an older Asian woman, aged fifty-three, five feet five and a slim 120 pounds. She likes nice cars, fancy French restaurants, and designer handbags. Her name? Lotus Flower.

I can't take my eyes off the image. It's a picture of Ahma.

How foolish of me to think that Ahma was meeting her dates at the gym! How so last century. No, not for this Modern Woman, rocking tight designer jeans and strappy stilettos. If Appa could see her now, he probably wouldn't even recognize her.

My anger doesn't completely obscure my humiliation at my public exposure. How dare setmeup.com use my private information for their marketing purposes? And my mother! I can't even imagine how she is going to feel when she finds out. I glance at the time displayed at the bottom of my computer screen. It is five thirty-eight. Ahma will be up in less than half an hour to lead her clients through weekend open houses. I pray that I can remove our profiles before anyone I know sees them. I log onto setmeup's website. I scroll down to the bottom of the home page and click on "Contact us." There is no phone number—only an email address. I click on help@setmeup.com and type the following message:

I was shocked to discover my personal profile being used to advertise your services. I did not give you permission to use my private information for your marketing purposes! The other picture is my mother. Please take down both pictures immediately!

I smash the "Send" button with my trembling, enraged finger. It is now five forty-five. I pray that setmeup.com has customer service on Sundays. I shower and get dressed, since there is no going back to bed for me now.

I hear Ahma turn on the sink on the other side of the house. It is a quarter past six. I check my email. There is a reply from setmeup.com. Incredible customer service. I open the message and read:

Dear setmeup Member,

As part of our registration process, every set-meup.com member is required to accept the terms of our standard online form agreement (the "Agreement"). Section 4.2 of the Agreement states as follows: "I hereby expressly agree, acknowledge and encourage setmeup.com to use any and all information that I contribute to the Website, including digital images, photos and my profile, for any purpose whatsoever, including for marketing, publicity and other public distribution. I hereby expressly relinquish ownership of any information that I upload and/or post to the Website and understand that such information becomes the property of setmeup.com in perpetuity."

As you can see from the above contractual language, you agreed to our Company's policy when you signed up as a setmeup.com member and clicked "I agree" to the terms of our electronic agreement.

Sincerely,
Customer Services
setmeup.com

P.S. I didn't realize that the pictures were a mother-daughter pair. That's quite catchy! Thanks for the heads-up!

I vaguely recall clicking on some agreement but don't remember reading any of the terms. I try a different approach:

Dear Customer Services representative,

Thank you for your timely response to my email. Does this mean that you do not plan to take down the ads of my mother and me?

Sincerely,
Alice Chang

I comb my soggy hair and blot it with a towel. I sit and wait. I hear Ahma get into the shower. I hit the "Refresh" button three times in rapid succession before a new email appears.

Dear Ms. Chang,

The profiles are part of our new marketing campaign and we believe that greater distribution to a wider viewer base will help our members successfully find mates! In fact, we believe this strategy will be so successful for our selected members that we envision that in the very near future, members will gladly pay for the extra visits to their profiles! Based upon your last email, we have made a few changes to our advertisement. Thank you for your input and we appreciate any suggestions you may have in the future.

Sincerely,
Customer Services
setmeup.com

I am impressed by their responsiveness, even though their response is not what I want. I switch computer tabs. My profile, and my mother's, are still prominently displayed, but the captions have changed. Above mine are the words: Lonely daughter . . . , and above Ahma's are the words that make up the rest of the question: . . . or lonely mama? Which one will you choose?

My scream brings Ahma rushing into the room. Her hair is wet, and she is wearing a bra and a linen skirt.

"What happened?"

I close my eyes. She rushes over to see what I am looking at. She sucks in air so deeply that she makes a whooshing noise like the closing of a bus door.

I open my eyes and peek at her out of the corners of my eyes. She is staring intently at our pictures.

"Why you use that one?" she asks. "Make your nose look flat."

"It was the best one I could find."

"You should ask me. I take good one. You like my one?"

"It's okay."

"I take myself."

She holds her arms straight out and makes an L shape with each hand, as though she is holding a camera. "Have to try five or six times. Not bad, huh?"

"Aren't you even embarrassed? Look at this! Right on the home page!"

"Why embarrassed?"

"Everyone can see that we're looking for dates!"

"That's the point."

"No, the point is for single people to find us, not the general public."

"Maybe married people have single friends." She pauses and tilts her head. "And maybe some single people too shy for internet dating. Why sign up if you want to hide?"

"Don't act like you're not embarrassed. I know you are! Otherwise, why didn't you tell me? You pretended that you met your dates at the gym!"

"Not for my embarrassment. For yours."

"What do you mean *mine?*"

Ahma sits down on my bed. Her pale stomach gently overlaps the waistband of her skirt, even though when she puts on her blouse and cinches her waist with a wide black leather belt, she will look as slender as a fashion model.

"You don't like me to date," she says.

"No . . ."

"You want me to be widow like long-ago days. You want me to wear only black clothes every day. You want me to suffer for the rest of my life. You want to punish me."

"No, I don't."

Ahma scrutinizes me with unblinking black eyes, and I have to confess, "It's not that I want you to suffer forever. I just want you to mourn, for a little while. You don't even seem to miss Appa."

My eyes fill with tears, but Ahma's face hardens as though someone has outlined her features with black crayon.

"I already miss your father when he was alive. I already suffer for that."

153

I blink my tears away so that I can see her more clearly, but Ahma has turned her attention and her gaze back to the computer, her manner now brisk and businesslike.

"Maybe we get more email now."

"I can't believe you aren't even bothered by this."

"Friends already know that we need date. Strangers don't know us, so doesn't matter."

"What about other people?"

Ahma shrugs, but then her face freezes in alarm. "Uh-oh. They know I'm liar."

I realize what she means. If I'm her thirty-nine-year-old daughter and she is my fifty-five-year-old mother, that means she had me when she was sixteen. "You could have been a teenage bride. From the old country."

She shakes her head. "Nobody believe that."

"What did you tell your dates that met me? Like Stephen and that guy from last night?"

"I tell them you thirty."

"And they believed you?" I ask, flattered.

"They can't tell. They think Asian people looks same," she says. "We have to ask them to take down before my clients see. Important for broker to be honest."

"I already tried. I sent them an email this morning, and that just made everything worse." I don't explain how, and she doesn't ask.

"No send email." She glances over at the clock. It is almost seven thirty. "Have to call. Personal contact most important. That's what head agent in training says to me."

Ahma clicks through the setmeup.com website, and I am surprised at her skill at maneuvering through the internal web pages. She clicks on links and jumps from page to page like a child skipping through a meadow. She finds the customer service number, displayed on the new member registration page but nowhere to be found on the customer support page, and scribbles it on a piece of paper. I head downstairs to eat breakfast while she calls setmeup.com from the upstairs telephone. By the time I've rinsed out my cereal bowl and put it in the dishwasher, she has straightened out everything.

"No problem. They have good customer service," she says, looking at her watch. "Even so early." In addition to wrestling with setmeup. com's customer service, she has also managed to blow-dry her hair, apply makeup, and finish getting dressed. "They say take down tomorrow."

"What? That's not what they told me."

"Personal contact," she says, nodding her head in agreement at her own statement. "Best way to solve problems."

After Ahma leaves, I crawl back into bed. Ahma handled everything so professionally. It's a side of her that I've been seeing more of since Appa died but that I rarely saw growing up. Is that what it was? Did he stifle her ambitions? What did she mean when she said that she missed my father when he was alive, that she had already *suffered for that*?

I try to lie still, but my legs feel jittery, and I rub the soles of my feet against the bedsheets. I don't recall my parents ever arguing. There was no drama in my house when I was growing up. My mother never threw dishes, and my father rarely even raised his voice. They didn't fight much, but did they love each other? I try to remember what they were like together. My memories are of me and my dad, or me and my mom. My dad taking me to the bookstore and letting me buy as many books as I wanted. My mom cooking dinner while I set the table. My dad taking me to school when I missed the bus. My mom shopping for back-to-school clothes and making me buy funny-looking pants because they were on sale. My dad coming home from work with a big smile on his face and a pack of gum just for me. But why can't I remember them holding hands, giving each other a neck massage or a hug? Stealing a kiss when they thought I wasn't looking? Where are the meaningful looks that I don't understand, the private jokes? Where are the adult conversations whispered above my head about things they don't want me to know?

What I remember instead is my father sitting at the breakfast table reading the newspaper while my mother washes dishes. My father eating dinner while my mother darts about in the kitchen. Why am I not able to conjure up memories of them doing something—anything—together? I can't recall a single family vacation when we were all together, but I know this can't be true. We took several car trips, but I can only remember being with one of them at a time. At Disneyland, I remember laughing with my mother as we twirled in a teacup on the Alice in Wonderland ride, but I can't remember where Appa was or what he was doing. I remember going to the Grand Canyon, and my father telling me that it was created by wind and water. I didn't believe him. How could wind and water carve rock? He explained that it happened over a long period of time, over millions and millions of years. It all adds up, he said, it's the nature of erosion. I looked down into the mile-deep canyon, striated with red that was also somehow gray, and green, and pink. I remember thinking that my father must have been mistaken, that this had to be the result of a meteor or the work of aliens, something more sudden and dramatic and catastrophic than the cumulative effect of wind against rock. I don't remember asking my mother what she thought, because I don't remember her being with us at all.

~

Ahma comes home around four o'clock from her Sunday open house. She is in good spirits. Her cheeks are flushed, and her eyes bright and shiny.

"Lots of offers today," she says. "So many."

"Really? Serious buyers?"

She laughs. "Not buyer! Date. Did you check?"

"No," I say.

She waves the back of her hand. "Go check. You probably get lots, too."

I log onto my email account.

"How many?" Ahma pops her head into my bedroom.

"Forty-seven."

She snaps her fingers downward and raises her knee. "Dammit!"

I turn to her, surprised.

"I only got thirty-five," she explains. "Good website. They know how to work." She leaves me to my messages and goes downstairs to make dinner.

I'm not sure whether Rick and I are exclusive, since we haven't had that conversation yet, and although I'm not interested in dating anyone else, I decide to keep my setmeup account, at least for now. Ahma is right. I have a lot more messages today. I spend the next hour scanning through them. About half of them sound sex crazed: "You and your mom are hot! My dad and I would like to meet you!" "Lotus Flower and Lotus Bud, I want both . . . ," "Alice, you look way younger than your mom and way hotter so I would pick you . . . ," but some actually seem okay: ". . . enjoy hiking and reading good books . . . ," ". . . ideal date is good books and strong coffee . . . ," ". . . favorite meal is brunch . . . ," ". . . write children's books and make wood furniture . . ."

By Monday morning, I have received a total of eighty-four profiles, and Ahma is prancing around the house with eighty-six setmeups in her inbox. Of these, I am still running at a rate of 50 percent loser/weirdos and the rest maybe normal. I still need to check the normal profiles against the ones that Ahma has. Any guy who is hitting on both the mom and the daughter is not anyone that either Ahma or I should ever meet.

Rick calls me that evening, seemingly unaware of my new status as Miss Popularity. He is at the airport, on his way to visit a client in Portugal.

"I already miss you," he says. I think of the night we spent at his house. Just hearing his voice on the phone makes my heart beat faster and my palms sweat.

"I miss you, too," I say, wiping my hands on my jeans.

After we end our conversation, Ahma pops into my room. She is in a chatty mood and sits down next to me on my bed. Now that we are no longer hiding our online dating from each other, we are free to share our dating likes and dislikes. I am surprised to hear that Ahma doesn't really care if a potential date is rich.

"Not poor," she clarifies. "No freeloader. But doesn't have to be rich. I can make my own money!" Her cheeks flush with pride.

"But your profile makes you look like a gold digger."

"Why?" She looks offended, even angry.

"All that stuff about designer handbags and fancy cars . . . it sounds like you're looking only for rich guys."

"But that's what I like!"

"That question isn't really asking you what you like. It's asking you to present an image of yourself."

"What?"

"You know, so people know what you're like."

"That's what I said."

"Oh, forget it."

"Why don't you add more?"

"More what?"

"Make you seem so boring. You like sushi and movie. Big deal." She rolls her eyes.

"What do you want me to do, lie?"

"No lie. Imagine."

"But I do like sushi and movie."

"Then you get boring guy. Do you want guy who like only sushi and movie? What about strong and handsome man with big brain? Maybe, like football and sudoku?"

Now it's my turn to roll my eyes.

"Up to you," she says with dramatic resignation, standing up to leave. "Your life."

ENDINGS AND
BEGINNINGS

CHAPTER FOURTEEN

I can tell there is something seriously wrong shortly after I arrive at the library on Tuesday. For one thing, Bertha hasn't touched her scone, although she slurps noisily at her iced caramel mocha. Elaine looks paler than usual and doesn't even glance up to say hello. They both look like they are about to cry.

"Good morning," I say cautiously.

They both look at me as though I have cursed in church. I settle into my station, put my purse underneath my desk, and boot up the computer. "Is everything okay?"

Bertha takes a loud sip of her drink.

Elaine shakes her head. "Sam isn't here again. He's not coming in for a while."

Mr. Park was absent all last week.

"He's never absent," she adds. "Definitely not for this long."

"When's he coming back?" I ask. "Is he sick?"

"Nobody knows. Sarah said that he's out indefinitely."

"Did he get fired?"

"No. But something happened to him. I could tell by the way Sarah looked when she told us. Something bad."

"Maybe he had an appendicitis attack?"

Bertha shakes her head. "Sarah would have told us that."

Sarah is the assistant head librarian and their immediate supervisor.

"Well, what did she say?"

"She said that Sam wasn't coming in for the rest of the month because something happened that she couldn't get into. But she looked like she was about to cry."

"Do you think he was arrested?" Bertha asks. Elaine and I stare at her.

"For what?" I ask.

"I don't know. You never know what anyone is really like. Maybe he was looking at kiddie porn on the internet."

My laugh is sharp. "Mr. Park? You've got to be joking."

"Or soliciting undercover cops disguised as teenagers in chat rooms."

"That's sick," I say, but then I remember my high school friend Megan, whose husband was arrested for doing just that, and I don't ask any more questions.

"You never know," Elaine says.

"I mean, do you ever really know anyone?" Bertha asks.

They look at each other with wide eyes. I don't believe that Mr. Park has been arrested for any internet crime involving teenagers, but there is no denying that something has happened to him, and whatever it is, it isn't good. I wish I could convince myself that the anxiety I feel is purely compassion for Mr. Park, but I can't help wondering whether something happened to Appa's notebook. If Mr. Park was arrested for something, would they have confiscated his belongings and taken the notebook, too? Nobody even knows when Mr. Park will be back, and I can't just sit and wait for him to return. Suddenly, I need that notebook more than anything. It is my only chance to know if my father meant to say anything to me, and to discover what I meant to him.

There is a chance that the notebook is in his office. I wait until Elaine and Bertha are on a break, and then I sneak down the hallway toward Mr. Park's office, trying to keep my stride even and purposeful. I turn the doorknob and am thankful that it's not locked. The door swings open. The lights are on. I walk in, glance at the papers stacked neatly on his tidy desk. If the notebook is anywhere in this room, then it would be in the desk's deep file drawer. This will only take a minute, but my heart is pounding like a jackhammer and I'm sure that Sarah can hear me all the way from the circulation desk. I walk behind the desk and pull open the drawer. I see hanging files but no notebook.

"Can I help you?"

A man's voice startles me. I turn my head and look up. He has dark-brown hair, dark eyes, and an angry expression. If I hadn't already been rendered speechless at being caught snooping, he would have taken my breath away. Even through the fog created by fear, I can see that he is gorgeous.

"I . . . I was . . . I was looking for something. Who are you?"

"I'm Victor. Mr. Park's son. Who are you?"

"Alice. I work with your father."

"What are you looking for?"

"A notebook. I gave it to him to translate."

His eyes narrow, but his expression softens. He no longer looks so angry, even though he still looks gorgeous. "Notebook?"

"It was in a yellow envelope."

His entire handsome face seems to dilate with comprehension. "It's not here. But I know where it is."

~

Victor has carefully written the directions on a sheet of paper, along with his phone number in case I get lost, but I manage to keep his green Subaru in sight as we weave through the quaint streets of Restin. I see him check for me in his rearview mirror, and he pulls over a couple of times when another car comes between us. We drive through the four blocks of downtown Restin, past the Cape Cod–style cottages, and up a steep hill to where the style of the houses changes to California

Craftsman. Mr. Park's house is one of the cozy ones, with a river rock chimney and a big wooden porch. Brightly colored perennials line the walkway. I feel a stab of longing for the life that I could be living if I were the type of person who got what she wanted. I turn off the engine and walk over to where Victor waits for me, on the flagstone walkway leading to my dream house.

The house is just as inviting inside as it is from the outside, with a pot rack and wooden floors, built-in cabinets, and original molding from the thirties.

"Did you grow up here?" I ask. He nods. He probably has no idea how envious I am. There is nothing flashy about the house. It is small by Orange County standards, and kind of dark, with no trendy upgrades or expensive furnishings. But it is exactly how I imagine my dream house. There is a red brick fireplace, which is not strictly necessary in Southern California, and the kitchen window overlooks the hills. I can see myself charmingly dusted with flour, taking a break from kneading bread dough to gaze out the window at the sunrise.

"Do you bake bread?" I ask.

He looks at me with an expression that is either puzzled or amused. "Usually it's Dad who does that, not me."

I nod.

"Do you live here, too?"

"Just this summer." He turns away from me and heads down a hallway. "I'll get your notebook."

I sit on the couch and gaze around the room. A comfortable-looking cracked leather chair is to my right. Books fill the built-in shelving. A stack of books is neatly placed on either side of the couch. Mr. Park apparently reads everything—I see biographies of celebrities and war heroes, short story collections, scholarly monographs. Framed photographs are scattered on the fireplace mantel. I get off the couch to take a closer look. There is a picture of Victor as a boy, about four or five. He had the same round brown eyes and thick brown hair that he has now, but as a boy, he looked like a different type of woodland creature, a bunny or a fawn, instead of the fox he is now. There is another picture, of a young Mr. Park with an arm around the waist of a woman with wild, feathered blonde hair. He is wearing jeans and a white T-shirt, and she is wearing a denim miniskirt and a striped tube top. Judging from their clothes and hairstyles, the picture was taken in the late seventies or early eighties, the time when *groovy* was shifting into *bitchin'*.

Victor returns, holding the large yellow envelope containing my father's notebook.

"Is this your mom?" I ask.

He nods.

"She's beautiful." She is, in a footloose, free-spirited way. "Your parents look very happy together." I remember too late that Mr. Park's wife recently died.

Victor eyes me carefully, as though he can't figure out whether I'm well meaning and just an idiot, or an insensitive busybody. I'm usually more respectful of other people's privacy, but I feel very comfortable with Victor, even though we've just met. Usually people this good looking make me nervous. But other than the first few minutes when he caught me snooping around his father's desk, he feels familiar, as though somehow we already know each other.

"Here you go," he says, handing me the envelope. This is my signal to leave, but I don't want to. I feel happy here, in Mr. Park's house, in my dream house. I want to know everything about the people who live here. I picture myself sitting in the leather chair, reading the Sunday *New York Times*. I can smell the baking bread.

"What does this house look like in the mornings when the sun comes up?"

He gives me a funny look, which I certainly deserve. Strangely, I have no qualms about asking Victor questions. "I don't know. I'm usually asleep."

"I bet it's beautiful. I bet the morning sun's rays make the room all orange." Victor just stands and stares at me, waiting for me to leave. But how can I leave when I want to live here?

"Can I have a glass of water? Then I'll have to hit the road."

No loud protestations from Victor at that. He practically runs to the kitchen, fills my glass from the tap, and hustles it back to me.

"The water is delicious," I say. "Is it filtered?"

"I don't know."

"The water probably just tastes better here." I take another long sip and look around. "You must do a lot of cooking," I say, glancing at the pot rack. This is *exactly* how my kitchen would look. In the mornings, orange light would stream in through the windows. I would putter around in fuzzy slippers with a cup of strong coffee, relishing the quiet before my family, including a friendly yellow Lab, awoke.

"I'll take your glass," Victor says.

I reluctantly hand it to him. I open the envelope and peek inside. "Was there anything else, besides this?"

"Like what?"

"Other papers? Your dad was going to translate this for me."

He shakes his head. "Just that, on his desk."

"I guess he didn't have time to get to it."

"What is that, anyway? My dad was always so absorbed when he was reading it . . ."

I look at the notebook in my hand. *This old thing?* "Something that your dad was supposed to translate. It's in Korean, and I don't read Korean . . ."

"Yeah, but what is it?"

"I don't know—that's why I wanted your father to translate it, so I could find out what it was."

He sighs, very slightly, but I hear it. I am being coy, and neither of us likes that. "Okay, I think it's my dad's diary. I dug it out of the garbage after he died."

"Oh. I see."

"I don't know what made me do it. I just couldn't stand the thought of it being thrown away. It's all that I have left of him." To my horror, I am suddenly crying. Victor puts one hand on my shoulder and helps me sit on the couch as though I am a very old, very fragile creature.

"I didn't even know that he kept a diary. I don't think I've ever seen him write anything other than a check. My mom threw all his stuff away . . ." I ramble this between hiccupping sobs, feeling relieved and unhinged at the same time. The sunlight warms the room, casting a glow on the mahogany walls and the wood floor. This is where I belong.

"Maybe that's better than hanging on to his things forever."

"Now you sound like my friend Janine," I say, although Janine is no longer my friend. "She always tells me to move on, get on with my life . . ."

"She sounds like me, talking to Dad about Mom. She died in January, but they had been separated for years. Dad just couldn't let go." He shakes his head. "I mean, just look at this place. It's like she's still here. Her pictures are everywhere. Her clothes are still in the closets."

"He must have really loved her."

"He still does. Unfortunately."

Then he tells me that his father is in the hospital because he tried to commit suicide. "I knew that he was depressed, but he's always been a little depressed, ever since Mom left him when I was in college. When I came home, I saw him lying on the couch with an empty bottle of wine next to him. I thought that was strange, since Dad doesn't drink much. He drank a lot after Mom died, and then he stopped. He'll have a glass with me sometimes . . ." His voice drifts, and he looks off into the distance. Sitting so close to him on the couch, I can see that his eyes are brown, but lighter than mine, almost golden in the center. "He wouldn't wake up. He had taken a bunch of sleeping pills."

"Is he going to be okay?"

"They want to keep him for a while, just to be sure." His eyes fill with tears. "I can't help worrying about how Dad will be when I'm in Nicaragua."

"Do you have to go?"

He shrugs. "A buddy of mine from college is counting on me. He made a fortune in software, and now he wants to pay it forward. He's starting these schools all over the world for kids who live in rural places. The kids are counting on me. It's something I've always wanted to do. Not this, necessarily, but something useful. It's why I trained to be an EMT. It's why I went to law school. I didn't want to feel like that anymore."

"Like what?"

"Like I was wasting my life. Like I wasn't contributing to anything. Every day that passed . . . I didn't want my life to be that. A bunch of days that had gone by too quickly, that just passed. I want to make something of them. I want them to count."

The blood rushes to my cheeks. His words are a rebuke to my very existence. What do I have to show for all my days? A failed marriage. No real career. No savings. No family of my own. I think of my aging ovaries, the precious egg that falls away every month.

"I keep trying to tell Dad. He's been walking around in a daze since Mom left—wasting the time he has."

"For how long will you be gone?"

"I'm not sure. A year at least. But now I'm not sure I should go at all."

He looks off into the distance again, and I know that he is thinking the same thing that I am. His mother . . . and now his father?

"How did your dad die?" he asks. For some reason, the question doesn't seem intrusive. I think he could ask me anything, and I'd be fine with it.

"They said it was stress-induced cardiomyopathy. Not sure what caused the stress. It was kind of sudden."

"Some people call it broken heart syndrome," he says, which I guess he knows from being an EMT. "It happens with old married couples. When one of them dies, the other one dies, too. Of a broken heart."

"My mom's still alive. She seems pretty happy, too."

He smiles. "Good for her."

We sit in silence until the light from the setting sun beams golden throughout the house, until it turns into the dusky rose of twilight. I guess it should feel awkward, but it doesn't. The thought crosses my mind that maybe I should leave, that maybe Victor wants to be alone. But somehow, I know that he doesn't, that he wants me to just sit with him, that my presence comforts him.

His phone beeps, startling us both. We must have fallen asleep on the couch.

"It's the clinic," he says. "I have to go."

"Let me know how he is," I say. We exchange numbers, and he promises to give me an update.

CHAPTER FIFTEEN

Victor is waiting for me in the lobby of the clinic where I was checked in after my hospital stay. I have been away from home for eleven days. My head aches, and I feel groggy. A weight presses against me from all directions, as though even gravity is working against me. I feel that soon I will be compressed into nothing, a mere cube the size of a gambling die. Victor stands when he sees me and walks over to take my hospital goodie bag, filled with my old gown, a small bottle of shampoo, and some sticky, overly fragrant lotion.

He gives me a hug in the middle of the waiting room, and I can only close my eyes with relief. He has not changed, it is only me. He reaches for my elbow, as though he fears that I might collapse before we make it to the car, and together we make our way to the parking garage.

When you are young, there are things that you do that will be blamed on youth. Indiscretions and impulsive behavior are expected. A failure to take risks can even be viewed as a character flaw. I know, because I was one of those children who was labeled as overly cautious, fearful, and—perhaps the worst of all—unadventurous. While my brothers learned to surf and dive off the cliffs of Maui, I stuck to the earth and cerebral pursuits. I spent sunny days on the floor of our modest childhood home, reading books too dull and dense for my siblings. They ran around the island shirtless and barefoot, kicking up dirt as children and, as teenagers, trailing broken hearts in their reckless wake. Perhaps it was their very wildness that calmed me, being the youngest of the three boys. I was not the baby of the family—that was my sister, Miki. Although we were only eighteen months apart, I anointed myself her caretaker and watched over her, ensuring that she didn't get trampled by her older brothers. My mother would shake her head at the latest recounting of her sons' misadventures and then say, "If it weren't for Sammy, I would think it's living on the island that makes the boys so wild!" I was proof that she made the right choice by staying put while so many of her friends married and moved to the mainland, to places like New York and Boston and Los Angeles, to high-paying, stressful jobs and what my father referred to as the "rat race." Whenever he said that, I imagined a bunch of rats underneath skyscrapers, wearing numbered jerseys and racing toward a finish line marked by cheddar cheese slices. The irony, of course, was that my brothers eventually settled down, having sowed their wild oats in their youth. They moved to the same neighborhood, married Korean Hawaiian women, and had beautiful children.

But not me. I married Crystal River and, in doing so, defied convention and parental expectation for the first time in my life. My reward was a lifetime of deceit and betrayal. Even the beautiful child I thought was mine belonged to another. Crystal River and I were cursed from the beginning, and our love—such as it was—was never meant to be in the form of flesh and blood. I should have known that there could be no living, breathing proof of a union that was based upon illusion and deception.

We had tried for many years, and I had resigned myself to a childless marriage. Why did I not find it strange that the miracle should happen after so many years? But our—their—baby did look like a combination of both of us. It had never occurred to me that she would take a lover who resembled me. Even later, when she stayed out all night and didn't explain, I never guessed that the men would look anything like me, and I suspect even now that they did not. Her other lovers were men she met at art fairs and bars, not at libraries. I pictured them with graying ponytails and tattoos, not broad Asian faces and hairless chests. But then, they were not substitutes for her true love. She already had me for that.

In the aftermath of reading something so painful, one does not think as clearly as one might. Instead, there are questions that need answers. The urgency to know overtakes rationality. It was in this state that I opened the medicine cabinet in search of the sleeping pills that I'd been prescribed several years ago when I suffered sleepless nights after Crystal River moved out. I swallowed seven without water, masochistically savoring the bitter taste on my tongue. Then three more with a dry white wine that I'd opened many weeks earlier and saved to use for cooking. The fruity notes had dissipated into the refrigerated air, leaving behind a stark medicinal flavor. I carried the bottle with me as I lay on the couch in our living room, lifting it to my lips and liking the out-of-control feeling that it gave me. I gazed at the picture of my wife and me in happier times. I could see so clearly the hunger in her eyes that I then mistook for vitality. I closed my eyes and waited for sleep. I wasn't trying to kill myself, as the doctor put it when she asked, "Were you trying to kill yourself?" No, I wasn't even thinking of myself, or death, or anything other than trying to reach Crystal River. I wanted to sleep, to dream of her, as her lover had done, and if that meant that my slumber needed to be eternal, so be it. It was one more sacrifice that I was willing to make. The mind is not rational in moments of great anguish, and I hadn't thought my actions through very clearly. I wanted to see her, if only for the last time. I wanted her to call to me as she had called to her lover.

But Crystal River never came.

~

"Are you awake?"

I lift my head and open my eyes. I realize that we are home, even though I have no recollection of being on the freeway or stopping at any traffic lights. My son—can I still call him my son, even if we share not a single drop of blood? Even though he could exist even if I had never lived?—wears dark sunglasses that hide his eyes. His profile is dramatic, like a movie star's. There are many girls who would follow him to his village in Central America. It is a miracle that he aspires to something greater than fulfillment of his physical and material needs.

I wait until Victor comes around to open my car door. He offers me his arm and grabs my hand with his own. I stumble on the gravel in the driveway, and his grip tightens around my hand so I do not fall. Like this, we head up the flagstone walkway together.

I sleep for two days. On the morning of the third day, I wake up ravenous. I walk into the kitchen, where Victor is eating cereal at the kitchen sink.

"Sit down," I say. "I'm going to make breakfast."

Victor puts his bowl in the sink and sits down at the kitchen table. He watches me as I crack eggs into a bowl and fry bacon in the cast-iron skillet. The bacon sizzles and spits, and it fills the air with a delicious smell that justifies the mess. When I set his plate before him, he waits until I have seated myself. He eats with a hearty appetite, even though it is his second breakfast of the day.

Afterward, I head for my study. Despite myself, I am anxious to find the notebook that I left on my desk. I do not yet know what I will tell Alice. Maybe I can tell her that I lost it? That it was in my backpack and somebody stole it?

The notebook is not on my desk, nor in my file drawers.

"Victor?"

He is putting away our breakfast dishes, drying them carefully with a towel and stacking them in the cabinets. He turns expectantly.

"Did you move anything from my office?"

"Just that yellow envelope with the notebook in it. A woman from your office said it was hers and needed it urgently for some reason." He turns away and continues drying the dishes. "I hope that was okay. It sounded important, and I wasn't sure how long you would be gone . . ."

I sense his discomfort and understand that he does not want to upset me during my recovery period. "It's fine. It was hers anyway. Alice, right?"

"Yes. We talked for a while. She seemed nice."

I have an unsettling feeling. "Did she stay long?"

"It was dark by the time she left, so I guess she must have."

"She doesn't talk much at work."

"Maybe she's different at work," Victor says.

Work. I put on the kettle to boil water for tea. I have decided to take a few weeks off work as personal leave. I have never done that before. Not even when my wife died.

"Dad?"

Dad. There is the possibility, isn't there, that he is really mine? Yet I know that I am only further deluding myself.

"Dad?"

"Yes," I say without turning around.

"Do you want me to stay?"

I don't answer him. The kettle whistles. I pour the water over the green tea leaves and breathe the fragrant rising steam.

"I don't have to go to Nicaragua. I can stay here, with you."

I turn and look at Victor. My son. Is he any less my son because we share none of the same genetic material?

The scent of green tea reminds me of the first time Victor tasted sushi. It was the first time Crystal River disappeared, and he was about twelve years old. I had a fierce craving for sushi and sake but was afraid to leave the house in case she called. I made a quick trip to the supermarket and bought a package of fish. A gleaming crimson salmon with white marbled fat. I had never made sushi before, although I had of course eaten it numerous times. I sliced the salmon into thin pieces, then strapped each piece with a band of nori to a mound of rice that I had splashed with rice vinegar. I made fourteen pieces of sushi that I arranged on a platter and carried triumphantly to the dinner table. Victor eyed my offering suspiciously. I poured sake into my coffee mug and green tea into a teacup for my son.

"Do I have to eat this?" he asked, looking at the sushi as though it might scuttle off the table.

"No. You can make yourself a peanut butter sandwich if you want."

He watched me take a piece of homemade sushi and dip it into soy sauce. I smacked my lips. Out of solidarity, he took a piece of sushi himself. He nibbled at one end and gagged.

"You don't have to eat it if you don't want," I said, taking another piece.

He watched me eat and drink and then, as if unable to watch his abandoned father eat dinner alone, he stuffed the rest of his piece of sushi into his mouth. He chewed quickly and then swallowed. Then he took another piece, and another, not even bothering to disguise the fishy taste with soy sauce.

That night, my stomach and my intestines rebelled. I spent half the time throwing up my dinner into the toilet and the other half spilling it out of my bunghole. The worst part was, I could hear my son having the same good time in the bathroom down the hall and I was too weak to help him.

The next morning, I stumbled into the kitchen to see him sitting at the table with his head in his hands. In front of him was a glass of fizzy liquid.

"How do you feel?" I asked.

He snorted and pushed the glass toward me. "It's for you. I already had some," he said. "It'll make you feel better."

I gulped down the liquid, which made me want to throw up again but eventually succeeded in settling my stomach.

"Dad?" Victor asks, bringing me back to the present. He is looking at me curiously, concern knitting his dark eyebrows together.

"Do you remember when I made sushi for you? When your mother disappeared the first time?"

Victor groans. "How could I forget? That was the worst case of food poisoning I've ever had."

"You didn't want to eat it. Why didn't you blame me?"

"What good would that have done?" He clutches his stomach in recalled agony. "That was not a good time."

"I think it was the chicken I had cut up for dinner the previous night. I used the same knife."

"It might have been the fish. It smelled . . . fishy." He wrinkles his nose, and I see him again at twelve, tall and bushy haired with gangly arms and legs. He is the same boy now, only filled out and serious. He seemed to grow up that night, as though he had thrown up his dinner and his childhood and flushed them both down the toilet. He never caused us any trouble. It was the other way around. He spent his youth watching over his parents.

"I didn't know that I was supposed to buy special sushi fish." I smile at him, and he grins back at me. "I'm sorry."

"It was a long time ago," he says. "My insides have recovered."

"No," I said. "Not only for that."

He looks out the window as tears fill his eyes. He wants to do good with his life, and I am so proud of him for that, for trying to make a difference, for continuing to have hope that what he does matters. I wonder when I stopped trying, when I stopped believing that I had the ability to change the world, or at least improve my small corner of it.

"It's okay, Dad."

"No. Not okay." How much more can I expect from him? I could cling to him and hope that he could save us both, but I would only drag him under with me. No, it's his turn now, and even though it hurts me to say it, I tell him, "Go. I want you to go. You will do much good there. I will be fine."

He nods. "You sure?"

I walk over to him and embrace him tightly. "I am fine, my son."

CHAPTER SIXTEEN

I pull open the glass doors to the Restin Public Library and brace myself for the blast of air-conditioning. The end of August is always the hottest time of the year. I make my way past the circulation desk and to the administrative offices in the back of the high-ceilinged room. Even though it is still morning, groups of kids are sprawled on bean bags or on their stomachs, reading books as though they share one big living room. I remember the library as one of my favorite summer retreats, flipping through back issues of *Seventeen* and *Teen* magazines, reading Beverly Cleary, and, later, skimming the racy scenes of Harold Robbins and Sidney Sheldon books.

When I get back to my desk, Elaine is grinning.

"Sam's back," she says. I already know this because Victor and I have been texting each other. Mr. Park's been on leave for over a month, but I am not supposed to know the reason why.

Bertha smiles and takes a big bite of a blueberry muffin. "He looks great," she says. Her red lipstick is peppered with crumbs.

"Does he . . . feel okay?"

"Yeah. We didn't ask. Sarah said to act normal. She didn't get into details."

"Oh."

"She said that he's a little depressed. Nothing criminal," Elaine says.

"Not that we really thought that," Bertha adds hastily.

"Of course not," I say.

When I get back to my desk, I check my phone. I have two messages. The first one is a voice mail from Rick. He is back in Portugal this week for work.

"Hi, beautiful. Wish you were here with me in Lisbon."

The second is a text from Victor, from Nicaragua. Just checking in.

I've been at my desk for only a few minutes when Mr. Park stops by our cubicles.

"Anybody need a sugar lift?" he asks. He is holding a bag of cookies.

"Sam, what did we ever do to deserve you?" Elaine asks, reaching for a snickerdoodle.

"For holding down the fort when I was out," he says matter-of-factly.

"Everything okay?" Bertha asks, taking a chocolate chip cookie.

"Yes," he says with such conviction that we all believe him. Then he turns to me. "I need to talk to you about payroll."

Elaine and Bertha are playful, glad to have Mr. Park back.

"Better go!" Elaine says, making a shooing motion with one hand and holding a cookie in the other.

"And make sure that he gives us juicy raises!" Bertha mock whispers.

I follow Mr. Park, feeling as though I have just been called into the principal's office.

"Sit down, sit down," Mr. Park says, gesturing to the chair across from his desk. I sit in the stiff chair with the scratchy fabric that looks like old carpeting. He sits behind his desk and pulls up a file on his computer. We review the payroll from the previous month, and he types in a few corrections.

"That way, IRS doesn't come after us," he says with a wink. I get up to leave.

"So I guess you met my son, Victor."

"Yes."

"I think he's quite fond of you."

"He's a very sweet . . ." I am about to say *kid* but then catch myself and say, "Person."

"He told me that you asked for the notebook back." He looks at me carefully. "I'm sorry I did not translate it."

"Oh, that's okay. I know you've . . . had other things to deal with. I didn't want you to have to read it when you were so . . . busy."

"Actually, I read all of it. But I did not wish to translate it."

He *read* it, but he did not *wish* to translate it?

"Why not?"

He frowns slightly and looks away.

"What does it say?"

He sighs heavily and then says, "It is a work in progress. Your father's private thoughts . . ."

His voice drifts off like smoke dissipating, and he suddenly seems very tired. His shoulders slump, and the skin on his face sags heavily. Although I am confused and upset by his behavior, I don't want to push, given what he's just been through.

"I should let you get some rest, um, get back to work," I say, and then slip out the door.

The exchange with Mr. Park has left me feeling off balance. He seemed cagey, or maybe he was just exhausted. What possessed me to give him my dad's notebook, anyway?

But I know. I did it out of desperation. And hope. Hope that I would gain some insight into who my father really was. Hope that it would reveal how much he loved me, *that* he loved me, despite his detachment.

Then a thought occurs to me. *Could Mr. Park be trying to protect me?* This would explain his strange behavior. Is there something in my father's notebook that he doesn't want me to know?

"Want a cookie?" Bertha asks, offering me the bag. I shake my head. She shrugs and takes another for herself. I want to grab the cookie out of her hand and tell her, "You can't keep eating these if you want to lose weight!" But then it occurs to me that maybe Bertha doesn't really want to lose weight. Maybe what she really wants is another cookie. Maybe what she really wants is for everyone else to accept her the way she is so that she can stop pretending to want to diet.

"I like your skirt," I say, gesturing with my chin. She looks down, as though she needed to be reminded of what she is wearing.

"Thanks. I got it at the mall. It's a size fourteen, but it's still a little tight . . ."

"It looks really nice on you."

~

The setting sun glows triumphantly across the sky, reflecting off my windshield and making it hard to see clearly, so it's not until I am at the house that I notice Janine's car across the street. I pull into the driveway and park. I get out of the car as she walks over to me.

"Hi," she says.

"Hi," I say, slamming the door shut. I am glad to see her, even though I try to hide it. It's as if we are in junior high school again.

"I thought I'd see if I could catch you. I know you're really mad at me, and I just wanted to apologize in person before you totally cut me out. I wouldn't blame you if you did."

I don't say anything. It makes me uncomfortable to see Janine so sincere and serious. We walk over to the front stoop and sit down, even though clouds of gnats are swirling around our heads in the twilight.

"I would invite you in, but my mom's home," I say.

"That's okay."

The brilliant tangerine sky softens to a pink mist.

"Remember Robbie Colt?" she asks suddenly.

"I still can't believe you slow danced with him."

Robbie Colt was the love of my life in the seventh grade, only nobody knew that except Janine. I made her swear up and down a hundred times that she would never tell anyone about my crush—literally a hundred. I made a scratch mark each time Janine recited, "I swear I won't tell another soul about Alice's crush on Robbie Colt," and I made a horizontal line across four marks every fifth recitation. As luck would have it, Robbie asked Janine to dance at the seventh-grade dance. She glanced apologetically at me and then took his hand and pressed up against him to a duet by Diana Ross and Lionel Richie.

"It seemed rude to refuse."

"And to 'Endless Love,' too. The most romantic song of the eighties."

We laugh. Remembering that time makes me feel forgiving.

"Boy, were you mad," she says.

"Yeah, I was." I gave Janine a tongue-lashing about loyalty and betrayal and then didn't speak to her for two weeks, an eternity when you are twelve years old. That's when we came up with our Rules of Friendship.

"He had wings," I say, remembering how his hair was layered around his face. "Plus, he could skateboard really well."

"I ran into him when I was in Seattle last year. He's the CEO of some lumber company up there."

"You should have held on to him. It might have worked."

Janine is silent. I look at her, and she is wiping her eyes.

"I'm sorry," she whispers.

"I really don't care about Jim."

She nods. "I know. He was an ass."

"I wonder what he's up to?"

"Nothing. He peaked early, and now he works as a bank teller or something."

"Figures."

"Are you still mad at me?"

"I think so," I say. "I don't really trust you."

"You never did," she says. We're both talking in a slightly joking tone, but we are both dead serious.

"Sure I did."

"I trusted you, too," she says.

"I'm sorry, too," I say. "I should have told him no. I didn't even want to go to the Homecoming Dance."

"But he was so cute."

"I never thought he was," I say. "But he was popular. I thought dating him would catapult us onto the A-list at Green Hills High School."

"So you were taking one for the team." She is smiling, and I know that she is no longer angry with me and I am no longer angry with her. Instead, I am overwhelmed with love for Janine, my oldest and dearest friend, who loves and forgives so easily and is willing to keep putting herself out there again and again. We know each other's weaknesses and flaws, and despite our acts of betrayal, we've always been there for each other.

"I should have asked you first," I say. "We should have had a conversation and decided together. We could have schemed our way to the popular clique."

"But we never did, and even now, we don't really talk about the big stuff. The really important stuff. Like why didn't you tell me that you were having problems with Louis? That's what best friends talk about. Marriage problems. Boy problems. When you don't share something that's so huge, it's almost like a betrayal."

I shrug. "I didn't realize we were having marital problems."

"But you must have. It's hard to believe that things are going great and then, one day out of the blue, he decides to ask for a divorce. That just sounds strange."

"We never fought."

"I just got frustrated. I'm sorry that I lost it with you."

"But you really believe it, don't you? The things that you said? That I'm dishonest and emotionally closed off."

183

"No. Yes. No."

I look at her, and she shakes her head. "No, I don't believe it. But yes, I do think you are not fully honest with yourself. Maybe I watched too much of that Oprah show growing up, but I think you are afraid of being emotionally vulnerable."

She looks tortured, her face blotchy and confused, and I think, *You are such a pain in the ass*, and I'm grateful for it. I'm glad I have someone in my life who expects more from me and who wants me to expect more for myself. I tell her then what I haven't admitted to anyone, even myself.

"I wanted to have kids and Louis didn't. I wanted to have them for a long time, and then everyone around us started to have them . . ."

"Except me."

"Except you, and I told him that I wanted to start trying. And you know what? He went and got a vasectomy. Without telling me. He said that he told me when we met that he never wanted to have kids, and he meant it."

"That's why you guys are divorcing?"

"No." I shook my head slowly. "That's why we got married."

"That makes no sense."

"I know. It was weird, tortured, guilt-ridden logic on my part. I tried to convince myself that it didn't really matter that I'd never have kids. Because he was right. When we met, neither of us wanted to have kids, and now I was changing the deal. And after he had the operation, I felt like I had to marry him because it was my fault, you know? He did it because he had me. I couldn't throw him back out into the dating world. Who would want him now? I mean, I know there are women out there who don't want kids, but it just reduces the pool."

"But you were only eighteen when you met. How could you know then whether you'd want kids later?"

"I know. It doesn't make sense when I explain it. That's probably why I never tried."

I'm the one crying now, and Janine puts an arm around my shoulder, and I lean my head against her, and we sit for a while in the twilight.

"Are you still seeing him?" I finally ask, raising my head. "The guy I saw you with at the sushi place."

"Stephen?" She nods, and an irrepressible smile zips across her face. "You're not mad, are you? Should I have asked you first? Did I break Rule Number Three?"

"Of course not. You don't need my permission. It's my mom you should be asking. She's the one who dated him, not me."

Janine looks at me, and a gnat flies into her open mouth. She spits it out and wipes her lips with the back of her hand.

"Did he tell you that *I* dated him?"

"He didn't say anything. But when he saw you at Zen Sushi, he started to act funny. I thought maybe you'd met online. I asked him if he knew you, and he nodded and said he didn't feel like talking about it."

"I don't blame him," I say, thinking of my mom's hairy-bear description of him. "Do you like him?"

"Yeah," she says. "I really do."

"Then good."

"But you don't seem to be doing too poorly yourself. That guy was really good looking. Is that Rick? The guy you met for coffee?"

I nod.

"Do you like him?"

I shrug. Janine looks disappointed, and I know that she thinks I'm keeping secrets from her again, which I am, in violation of Rule #1.

"Have you two . . . ?"

I look at her and smile. She laughs.

"And?"

"He's too good looking and too rich."

"How awful for you."

"I know, but the thing is . . . there's someone else. I just met him. His name is Victor."

"On setmeup?"

"No. He's the son of a guy I work with at the library."

"The son?"

"The guy I work with is sort of old."

"How old is he?"

"I don't know, sixty or seventy or something. I can't tell."

"No, his son!"

"I don't know, about twenty-five?"

"Twenty-five!"

"Wait, no, I think he's twenty-six?"

Janine purses her lips, widens her eyes, and raises her eyebrows.

"I don't mean it like that. We talked and understood each other in a weird way. I felt really comfortable with him. It was like being with Louis."

"So basically, you want to skip the exciting, passion-filled courtship phase and just go straight to the boring-ass marriage. Or why not just skip straight to the midlife crisis divorce?"

"I could do that."

"What's wrong with Rick, again?"

"Nothing. Maybe that's it. There's nothing wrong with him. He's smart, he's handsome, he's polite. But he makes my palms sweat, and I can't really relax around him because my heart is beating so hard. He throws me off and makes me feel awkward."

"You have a mad crush on him."

"It feels like stress."

"That's how you're supposed to feel when you're attracted to someone."

"Then how come he doesn't act that way around me?"

"You think maybe he's not into you because he doesn't have sweaty palms?"

I shrug. "Maybe he likes me okay. But I don't think he's crazy about me. Isn't he supposed to be nervous around me? I mean, if he really liked me?"

Janine shakes her head and then presses her palms to her temples like she has a horrible migraine. "He could just be that kind of guy. You know, the kind that knows how to handle himself? The kind that has his act together?"

"The kind that isn't super crazy about me?" I can feel my mouth turn down, like I'm going to cry again. Although I have never said it in so many words, Janine knows my biggest fear is ending up in a relationship without passion, like the one I saw growing up, like the only one I've ever had. "I guess I don't know what I want. I don't know what a good relationship is supposed to look like. Why does it always feel like you have to pick? Passion or stability? Romance or companionship?"

"Hot sex or good conversation?"

"Comfort or excitement?"

"Lust or like?"

"Friends or lovers."

"Joey or Chandler?"

We look at each other and start laughing, and this makes us each laugh even harder, until both of us are laughing so hard that we are doubled over, tears rolling down our cheeks.

"How old are we, anyway?" she asks. "Look at us. We're nearly forty years old."

"Don't remind me."

"And we still don't know what we want. We haven't changed all that much since seventh grade and Robbie."

"And look at him now. He's the CEO of some big company."

"With four kids."

"Robbie has four kids? You never told me that!"

"I didn't want to upset you. His wife looks like a model, too."

"Who would have guessed in high school that this is where we'd be at forty?"

"The question is," she says, "where are we going to be at fifty?"

"Hopefully not at El Toreador."

~

Ahma is talking on her cell phone at the kitchen table when I finally come inside. She acknowledges my existence with a glance and then continues talking. I open the fridge and peer inside, wondering whether there are any tasty leftovers. Ahma motions frantically to get my attention, flapping a hand like she is putting out a fire. She points to a foil-wrapped container on the counter. I nod. The bindaeduk is still warm. I take two of the mung bean pancakes and place them on a plate and pour a little soy sauce and white vinegar into a sauce bowl. I carry the plate and the bowl to the kitchen table. Ahma has already set the table for me with a pair of chopsticks, a paper towel thriftily torn in half, and a glass of water. I eat while she closes another deal. She hangs up the phone as I am taking my last bite of bindaeduk.

"Want more?" she asks, getting up.

"No, no! I'm full," I say, patting my stomach. "It was really good."

"Not too spicy?"

"No."

"Taste is better fresh."

"It was still warm."

"But soggy. You have to eat it fresh from pan. Do you want me to warm it up?"

"No, it was good." I used to resent my mom's pushiness when it came to food, especially when I was in high school and on one of Janine's *Teen* magazine diets. Now I try to accept it as her way of expressing maternal love.

"Why you are late?"

"I was talking to Janine. We were outside."

"How come didn't come inside?"

"She had to go somewhere. We didn't mean to talk so long."

"She's good friend. Longtime friend."

"Yeah. She is."

"Marry yet?"

"No. But she's dating someone."

"Oh, good."

"Who were you talking to just now?"

"Broker."

"Did you sell another house?"

She nods. "Big house. Two million dollars."

"Wow!"

Ahma looks pleased but allows herself only a hint of a smile. "Buyer want some free things. Free curtains. Free doormat. Two-million-dollars house and buyer want to save two hundred." She shakes her head.

"That must be some commission."

"I make more money now than your father."

"The housing market is good right now," I say.

"Up and down," my mom says. "Never predict future. Even tomorrow. Maybe buyer change mind. Have to be at office very early. Buyer from New York. Very rich."

"Good for him," I say. "And for you."

"Not him. Rich lady. Young, too."

"Good for her."

"What does he do?" Ahma asks as she walks up the stairs.

"Who?"

"New boyfriend of your friend."

"Oh, him. I'm not sure. He's some kind of doctor," I say.

"Good," says Ahma. "She need doctor. Somebody take care of her."

I am tempted to tell her just who Janine's doctor boyfriend is, but I bite my tongue. I have changed since the seventh grade, even if I'm not a CEO with four kids.

CHAPTER SEVENTEEN

Some people think that there are no seasons in Southern California because the changes are subtle, the transitions smooth. In late September, the sun rises lazily and shines gradually rather than blazing boldly and brightly as it does in the summer. The days, although shorter, continue to be sunny and warm, but the mornings and evenings are cooler. I can finally wear my favorite sweater. A few trees change color, although many stubbornly remain green until they suddenly lose their leaves in December, like an old lady who manages to fool her neighbors with plastic surgery and then drops dead, revealing her true age. I can't help thinking about death—and life—as I make my way through the late-morning commute to Restin. Death and life, life and death. Two ends of the same spectrum.

The subject isn't purely metaphysical. I am nearly three weeks pregnant.

That's technically incorrect. I'm probably five weeks pregnant, if you count it the weird way doctors do when they are trying to figure out the delivery date. I learned this online as I was researching all the possible reasons for missing a period: stress, obesity, low body weight, a thyroid issue. But the most common reason is pregnancy.

Still, what were the odds of me getting pregnant? Rick and I are still seeing each other, but erratically, because he travels a lot for work. We had sex only once without a condom. It was early in the morning, and protection was not something either of us was thinking about. Anyway, I am almost forty years old. That means I am of "advanced maternal age," and even if I were trying, it would be highly unlikely. But I bought a home pregnancy test anyway, feeling foolish and half expecting to get my period while I was in line waiting to pay for it. I was sure my body was just overreacting to the newly awakened sensation of being with a man, but then I saw the second blue line creep across the window.

I haven't told anyone. Not my mom or Rick when he called last night. It's still early. Anything can happen.

I park next to Bertha's PT Cruiser. I glance inside as I lock my car door. The interior is immaculate, like a brand-new car. No loose tissues on the floor or empty water bottles on the back seat. The outside of her car looks newly washed and gleams, not like mine, with its dirty windows and the white bird droppings that have hardened like plaster on the roof. I don't see Mr. Park's Prius in the parking lot.

Bertha and Elaine are both busy at their computers. Bertha is checking her personal email, and Elaine is buying clothes online.

"Two dates for this weekend," Bertha says to me triumphantly. "I am soooo glad that you told me about this website. What about you?"

Although I am happy for her, I am not crazy about the competitive side that has emerged now that she thinks we are dipping into the same pool of available men.

"Nothing," I say. I haven't told her about Rick or that I've taken down my setmeup profile. She squelches a smile but manages to knit her eyebrows into a semblance of sympathy. I suddenly feel very light headed. I sit down and close my eyes. The room spins. I lay my head on my desk.

"Are you okay?"

I turn and open my eyes. At first, I am not sure what I am looking at. A brown marble, or is it a bug with black legs? Then my vision clears like a lens being adjusted, and I realize that it is a makeup-smudged brown eye belonging to Bertha.

"Are you okay?"

Bertha is bent over, her face less than an inch from mine. Elaine is standing behind her.

"Did I just pass out?"

"I'm not sure. If so, it was only for a second."

I stand up and then sit back down. My head is spinning.

"I just . . . haven't had anything to eat . . ."

A scone magically appears in front of me. I take a bite. I guess I really am hungry. I polish it off. I start to feel much better.

"Thanks for the scone. I think I just had low blood sugar."

"It happens," Bertha says.

My phone buzzes. It's a text from Victor, from Nicaragua. We have been texting regularly. I'm kind of a spy for him. I give him regular updates on how his father is doing to reassure him. He texts Mr. Park, too, of course, but it's not the same as seeing him. When his father doesn't answer the phone or respond to his texts immediately, Victor imagines the worst. I guess I would, too, after what happened.

Worried about Dad again. Can you please check on him?

Of course.

Thanks. I owe you.

No problem.

"I have to go talk to Mr. Park about something," I say. "Do you know where he is?"

"He's not in today," Bertha says.

"Where is he?"

"He wasn't feeling well, so he stayed home today. He's probably checking email."

I think about Victor's text. What if Mr. Park isn't okay?

"I'm not feeling great myself." I clear my throat and cough carefully. "Something might be going around."

Bertha scoots her chair, just barely, away from me. "Maybe you better go home if you aren't feeling well."

"Yeah. Better to be safe than sorry."

I remember that I have to drive through downtown Restin, but I'm not as confident about the rest of the way to Mr. Park's house. I guide myself using the crinkled piece of paper with Victor's handwriting on it, glad that I saved it in the glove compartment instead of throwing it away. I remember following his green car, and Victor checking in his rearview mirror to make sure that I wasn't held up by a red light, and pulling over to the side of the road to wait for me when I got cut off by another car.

I take a turn up one of the hills right off Main Street and follow the gentle curves. I pray that I am not too late. I turn a corner, and then I see it. The cozy wooden porch with the river rock chimney and the flagstone walkway. I see both Mr. Park's Prius and Victor's Subaru parked in the driveway. I pull up to the curb in front of the house and rush up the walkway.

I was so preoccupied with finding my way here, and so worried that Mr. Park might have harmed himself, that I didn't have a chance to think about what I would say to him. When he opens the door, I can only stare at him.

"Mrs. Markson," he says, looking alarmed.

"You're okay," I say, equally surprised. Then I quickly add, "Actually, it's Ms. Chang. My divorce is going to be finalized in a couple of weeks."

"Oh, I'm sorry to hear that," he says. Then, uncertainly, "It's a pleasant surprise to see you."

"Are you . . . is everything okay?"

Mr. Park looks at me. "Why do you ask?"

"I—I was just concerned when you didn't come in to work today and . . ."

The skeptical look on his face makes me stop and confess, "Okay, Victor asked me to check on you. He texted me from Nicaragua. But he didn't ask me to check on you at home, just check on you at work, but then you didn't come in to work, and so that made me panic—"

"I shouldn't have worried him. Or you."

"I just wanted to make sure, because I promised him."

"So, you've been communicating with my son often?" He says the words slowly, deliberately.

"We text."

He frowns slightly.

"He's just concerned about you, that's all. He wanted me to make sure you were okay, since he's not here."

"Do you plan to stay in touch?"

I am not sure what he means by this. Is he going somewhere?

"I'm not going anywhere," I say. "Are you?"

"I mean with my son."

"I-I guess so."

"You seem to have hit it off. He seems to be quite fond of you as well."

"Victor's great," I say. "We seem to understand each other. Too bad he's in Nicaragua. I think we'd be hanging out all the time. We probably will when he gets back."

He is staring at me and standing very still.

"Is everything okay?" I ask.

He blinks, and I wonder if he is about to have a heart attack. I brace myself, ready to catch him if he falls.

"I have to tell you something that might come as a bit of a shock to you," he says. "I know it came as quite a big shock to me." He stares at me for a very long moment. Then he opens the door wider to invite me inside.

CHAPTER EIGHTEEN

Alice, formerly Markson but now Chang, follows me into the house, and I motion for her to sit down on the leather chair. When the doorbell rang, I thought it might be Walt Moroney from down the street, returning the rake he borrowed earlier in the week. The last person I expected was Alice Chang.

"Would you like some tea?" I'd made a fresh pot and had just settled with a nice cup of *sencha* into the very seat in which she is now sitting when the doorbell rang.

I am playing hooky from work today. I planned to indulge in a day devoted to drinking tea and reading a historical novel. At my age, it's important to take whatever pleasures I can. I was feeling rather despondent this morning, and the idea of work overwhelmed me. In the past, I would have chided myself for my self-pity and gone into the office anyway. But given everything that's happened, I have resolved to be kinder to myself, to indulge my needs once in a while.

"Sure, I would love some tea. Thank you," Alice says. Her eyes dart around the room, and she looks young, which has more to do with her manner than anything else.

I bring back a cup of green tea from the kitchen and hand it to her. She thanks me and cradles it between her hands without taking a sip. She sits and waits expectantly. I seat myself on the couch next to the leather chair.

"You and my son seem to have a special connection."

She looks at me and slowly turns red.

"I don't mean to embarrass you."

"He's very nice, but there's nothing going on between us, if that's what you mean."

"Things have a way of changing. What you think is one thing can shift into something else."

"And you want to make sure that doesn't happen?"

"You misunderstand me."

She looks surprised. "Then you want me to get together with him?"

"No!"

"Then?"

"Please do not take it personally. It's simply that . . . it can never happen."

She looks at me, visibly annoyed and then puzzled.

"I have to tell you something," I say, "but I am not sure how you will react. I must tell you so that you will understand."

She takes a slow sip of tea and then nods.

"Victor is your brother. Your half brother."

She laughs. "You're joking, right?"

"I'm afraid not."

"How do you know?" she asks, and then her eyes widen.

I nod. "Your father had a love affair with Crystal River, my wife. It's in his notebook."

I tell her about the yearslong affair between her father and my wife, how they met in Korea and then again in Los Angeles. I keep it as brief as possible, sparing her unnecessary particulars. There is no need to tell her about the first time her father got Crystal River pregnant, when they were teenagers in Korea. But

I must tell her about the second time, and how my wife's pregnancy ended their affair and gave me a son. I try unsuccessfully to control the bitterness in my voice, a bitterness that reveals what I do not say: *They never stopped loving each other.*

"Did my father know she had Victor? Did they see each other again?" she asks. "I want to know everything."

"What do you mean?" I ask, but I know what she means. She wants to understand the unfathomable. I have felt this same desire, and that is why I am certain that she does not really want to know *everything*. She does not want to know about their youthful meetings, their assignations in hotels, his dreams of my wife. She does not want to know about her father's regret or his disappointment with his life. She does not want to know about the passion he had for my wife, or the cruel thoughts he harbored about her and her mother. In the darkest hours of the night, my words would haunt her; they would eventually destroy her the way her father's words almost destroyed me.

"Who ended their affair?" she asks. I know what she means: *Did he choose us over her?* But I can neither lie to her nor tell her the truth.

"Your questions have no answers," I say. "They will only lead to more questions. It is better that I tell you nothing more."

She nods, frowning slightly. She doesn't say anything for a long moment, sitting very still, immobile except her facial features, which now shift as her thoughts race through her mind, each thought altering her expression like one frame clicking seamlessly into the next to create a narrative arc. Her mother's unhappiness, her father's detachment, the starved marriage they must have had. My suicide attempt, the bond between her and Victor. The genetic recognition that she might have mistaken for compatibility or intimacy.

"Are you okay?" I finally ask.

"This explains a lot."

"You understand now why I didn't want to translate the notebook? And why I need to tell you now?"

She nods. "Does anyone else know?"

"No."

"Not even Victor?"

I shake my head.

"Do you plan to tell him?"

"I don't know." After a moment I add, "Do you?"

She shakes her head. "No. That is your secret to tell." She adds, almost matter-of-factly, "I don't think it will make a difference to him."

She means that Victor will not care that I am not his biological father. I know that what she is saying is probably true. I know this in my head, but I am not sure I know this in my heart.

We listen to the birds chirping. The hum of the refrigerator.

"I have a secret of my own. Do you want to hear it?" she asks after a while. I don't say anything, but she tells me anyway. "I'm pregnant."

"Pregnant?"

"You're the first person I've told," she says. She notices the look on my face and smiles despite herself. "Don't worry. It's not Victor's."

I breathe a quiet sigh of relief. "Then, your ex-husband's?"

She shakes her head. "Someone else."

"You haven't told him?"

She shakes her head. "I guess I want to figure out what I want to do first. I've always wanted to have kids, but my husband—my ex-husband—couldn't have any. And I don't want to rush into anything with Rick—he's the guy—just because I want to have kids. Plus, I haven't even decided whether I want to keep it. But this might be my last chance to be a mother."

"Do you think you could be a good mother?"

"Yes. I think so. I want to be. But I'm not sure how I would do it without being with him. Being a single parent sounds so hard. And I don't even have my own place. I live with my mom . . ."

"Will your mother want to have a baby in the house?" Although I have never met Alice's mother, I have great compassion for her. We have so much in common, and I do not wish her to suffer anymore.

She shrugs. "I don't know."

I stand and walk into the kitchen with the pretense of freshening my cup of tea. I need to think without being distracted by her anxious presence. I don't believe in fate, but I do believe in opportunity. Just yesterday, I received another newsletter from HANA, the nonprofit in Hawaii that I have been donating to for years. The ad for an archivist was still listed. It has been over forty years since I was last in Hawaii, that long since I saw my own parents. Crystal River had created a rift so deep that by the time I admitted to myself that my parents were right, years had passed. But it is never too late to go home.

I return, carrying my replenished cup of tea. "You can stay here."

"Where?"

"In this house. If you want."

"With you?"

"No. As much as I like babies, I can't stand to hear them cry. Especially at three in the morning."

"Where would you go?"

"Back home. To Hawaii. While both my parents are still alive. They are very old."

"Will you come back?"

"Probably. It's likely. But nothing is certain."

"I appreciate this, but I need to think about it. I'm not sure I could—it's quite generous . . ." Her voice trails off, and I suspect that she is wondering how much I would charge for rent.

"It's your choice. You can stay here, whether you decide to keep the baby or not. I need someone to house-sit, that's all. Unfortunately, I could not pay you. It is a lot to ask of you, and all I could do in return is provide you with a place to stay. But I need somebody to take care of the house while I am away. Somebody needs to water the hydrangeas."

She shakes her head. "It's so incredibly generous of you."

"You would be doing me a tremendous favor."

"Are you kidding? This is my dream house."

"Then it's the least I can do for the half sister of my son."

She sits quietly, thinking. Imagining, perhaps, the many paths her life could take. Finally, she says, "I feel like I'm forcing you to leave your own house."

"No," I say. "You are giving me an opportunity that I have been too timid and unimaginative to take. You are giving me the chance to restart my life."

"Then it's a chance for us both."

After Alice leaves, I remember something. I walk into Victor's bedroom, which has remained virtually unchanged since he left. I had packed some of his things in boxes. He didn't have much. His bed is made and his books are still on the bookshelf. I peer underneath his bed. It is dark and I can't see anything. I get on my knees and feel around with my hands. I scrape my fingers on a surface rougher than sandpaper. I pull out the lava rock. It is heavier than I remember and looks bigger, too, as though it has grown with the passage of time. I carry it to the kitchen, where I set it down on the table. I rinse my hands underneath the tap water and then apply antiseptic while I call the airline and make reservations. I will go to Kona first, to return the rock, before heading home.

CHAPTER NINETEEN

The morning sickness has subsided somewhat, but my body is still uncomfortable. I see myself in the mirror, and what I see is both the same and different, like everything else in my world. What I thought I knew turns out to be . . . not wrong, but incomplete.

I remember the morning when the tow truck came for my father's Audi, and how my mother had tossed his belongings for curbside trash pickup. I mistook my mother's actions for disloyalty, for coldness. Now I understand her abbreviated mourning period differently—her new job, her new wardrobe, her dates. Instead of spending the rest of her days steeped in regret, she is reclaiming the narrative of her life, changing its meaning by changing its ending.

And Victor. The instant connection. The trust we felt. The familiarity that I might have mistaken for something more if it hadn't been for Rick, who showed me what it feels like to have someone light your fire. I understand that now, too.

I have a sibling. A brother. I am no longer an only child. I am not quite sure what that will mean, but I know it will at least mean that Victor, and Mr. Park, will always be part of my life in some way. And part of my baby's life, because I have decided to continue my pregnancy.

I have thought about this for weeks, uncertain of the right thing to do. What kind of a mother will I be? How will I manage when I can barely manage taking care of myself? But stronger than all these worries is my desire. *I want this baby*, so much that I wonder whether I have ever really wanted anything before in my life. The questions I ask myself are not ones that I can answer now. Instead, I must trust myself, believe that I can do this, because this is my life, and it is time I started to live it. Maybe it's not the life or the family that I thought I would have—or that I thought I did have—but it is the life and the family that I want. It is like solving a puzzle that I have been trying to figure out my entire life, and it is only now, after the last piece has clicked into place, that I can see the whole picture clearly. This strange new world has helped me make sense of the old one. This strange new world makes more sense than the old one.

I am going to have a baby. The thought of it still astonishes me. Even though I have not yet told Rick that I am pregnant.

~

Rick has to work late, so we agree to meet at the Thai restaurant near the beach. I have resolved to tell him tonight. When he sees me, he gives me a quick kiss hello on the lips. I feel light headed and regret not having had a more substantial snack before meeting him. I have gained seven pounds since our first date and wonder whether he notices, but then I think, *Of course he must notice.* I self-consciously tug on my shirt to cover my expanding rear. The hostess seats us at a small table in the back, where it is quiet. The waitress brings over glasses of water. I gulp mine down gratefully. My hands are clammy and trembling, and I clasp them in my lap so that Rick won't notice.

"It's so nice to be back home," he says. "It never fails. Whenever I come back from a business trip, I appreciate how lucky I am to call this place home." He waves his hand around, meaning the beaches and the weather outside, and not the bamboo furniture and the dim lighting inside the restaurant. He reaches over and takes my hand, which is damp and limp.

"I'm pregnant," I blurt. This is not the best way to break the news to him, but I feel my resolve slipping away. If I don't jump into the cold pool of confession, I am afraid I'll chicken out.

He looks at me with a slight smile on his face, which fades away when he realizes that I'm serious.

"And it's yours," I add, just in case he is thinking of saying something hurtful.

"Are you sure?"

"That it's yours?"

"That you're pregnant."

"What do you think?"

"I'm sorry," he says, pulling back his hand. "I'm just surprised. But I guess it only takes one time."

We sit in sullen silence. I'm not sure whether he's angry at me or whether I'm angry at him. Maybe both. Maybe neither.

"I'm sorry," he says again.

"For what? Getting me pregnant?"

The waitress appears at our table and patiently waits for our order. We randomly pick something, and she leaves.

He takes a long sip of water, and I resist the urge to rest my head on the tablecloth and fall into dark unconsciousness.

"So what are you going to do?" he asks.

We exchange a long look. I can't tell by his expression whether he is hopeful or afraid, or of what he might be hopeful or afraid.

Finally, I say, "This might be my last shot. I'm almost forty."

He nods. "This could be the last shot for me, too."

"Hardly. It's different for men."

"Not really. Haven't you read those articles about the risks of aging men's sperm?"

"Listen, you don't have to feel obligated. I'm perfectly capable of raising a child on my own."

He nods, his face a blank. I am totally lying, and he knows it.

"I don't think we should rush into anything," I say.

"It's a little late for that."

"Okay. But you know what I mean."

"You don't want to rush into a relationship, but you want to have a child together," he says.

"It sounds like you don't want that."

"I didn't say that."

"Then you want me to have this kid but not be together?"

"Is that what you want?" His tone is even, and I can't read his expression. His demeanor is as calm and cool as ever. Neither of us is willing to show our cards, but he is doing a much better job of hiding his. Maybe he is fine with having a baby. Maybe he just doesn't want to be stuck with *me*. Or maybe he doesn't want me to continue the pregnancy. Maybe he does but wants nothing to do with a baby *or* me.

But then I see what, if we were playing poker, would be his tell. His right thumb is nervously flicking his right index finger. Flick, flick, flick. Now I know that he is as uncertain and confused as I am. I feel a little better.

"No. I don't want to rush into anything . . . but I do want to have this baby. Other than that, I don't know." How could I know when we haven't known each other very long?

"We can see how things go," he says. "I don't know what's going to happen. But I do know that I like spending time with you."

"I don't want you to feel like we or you or I have to . . ."

"I know. And we don't, either of us, have to do anything or be in anything that we don't want to be in, especially since we've both just gotten out of long-term relationships."

"So what are you saying?" I ask.

"What I'm saying is, I don't think we have to know everything right now, do we? We can just see how it goes." Flick, flick, flick.

I let my breath out slowly, not realizing until then that I have been holding it. Like a valve, his words relieve the pressure that I have been carrying since our first date, a pressure whose origin I haven't until now understood. I don't have to know how this story will end in order to begin it. I think of Ahma, who had thought of her life as one thing and then discovered it was something else entirely. The ending is not at all what she expected, but she can make it one that she wants.

"But there is something that I am going to ask for," he says. "If you are going to have this baby, *our* baby, then I want to participate. I want the chance to be a father. Even if you decide that you don't want me for your husband." As he speaks, he looks right into my eyes with such a serious expression that I feel a funny sensation deep in my stomach, as though the earth has suddenly dropped away, then quickly shifted back into place to catch me. I suddenly have the urge to run my fingers through his hair and wrap my legs around him.

"So, one step at a time," I say.

He nods. "One step at a time."

~

My conversation with Rick has given me enough courage to finally tell Ahma that I am pregnant. When I do, she just stares at me as though she is trying to read my lips.

"Who's father?" she asks, after a long moment.

"You don't know him."

"You get marry?"

"I don't know. Maybe in the future. Maybe not."

Rick offered to let me move into his beautiful house, but that doesn't feel right. It would be too easy to slip into something then, too hard to leave. I don't know what will happen with us, only that we have decided to remain in each other's lives. There is no road map for what we are doing, only the next step in whatever direction makes the most sense and feels right.

Ahma takes a sharp sip of air, and then she starts to cry. I was not expecting that. I was prepared for her to get angry, to call me all sorts of nasty names. But I was not expecting her to cry.

"You keep baby?" she finally asks. I nod. She's always wanted me to have kids, but not like this. Still, I have to move forward with my life and stop paying for my parents' unhappiness with my own. She may not understand my decision, but I hope that she will forgive me for it.

She sits quietly for a very long time, and I am too upset to move. I think that if I try to stand, my bones will crumble to dust.

"Good," she whispers. "Almost too late for you."

I turned forty the week before. It was a quiet celebration. Just dinner and cake with my mom and Janine, who had come over to share her good news. She had just gotten engaged to Stephen.

"I know you want baby ever since you were little girl," she says, putting out her hand, palm-side down, at waist level. "Always play mommy. Like mommy was something special."

"It is special."

She doesn't say much to me about my pregnancy after that, although frankly, I don't see much of her the next couple of weeks. She is pretty busy with all her setmeups and work. I start to pack, just a few boxes. Ahma doesn't ask me about the packing, and I delay telling her about my plans to move. I thought she would be relieved not to have to put up with a crying newborn at all hours of the day and night. But when I finally tell her, she looks hurt.

"What if you have emergency?" she asks.

"I have a phone."

She frowns. "Why not stay here?"

"I want my own place. I'll feel more comfortable. And Mr. Park needs someone to look after his house while he's away."

She nods. It is easier for her to accept my leaving if she can believe it is only because I am doing somebody a favor.

CHAPTER TWENTY

"Ay! Ay! Ay!" Ahma scolds, roughly pulling the last box out of my arms even though she is already carrying a large shopping bag around one wrist.

"It isn't that heavy," I say, but she hisses angrily as she trips up the flagstone walkway in her heels. I unlock the door and let her into the house. Ever since I've started to show, Ahma has treated me as though I were made of glass. Even though I am only in my fifth month, my regular clothes no longer fit, except the occasional drawstring skirt or oversize sweatshirt. Against my wishes, Ahma went out and bought maternity clothes that are more stylish than anything I am used to wearing.

"Supermodel design," she says, handing me the oversize shopping bag. I must admit that she has good taste. Inside the bag are two Empire-waist jersey knit dresses, two pairs of black stretch pants, a denim skirt, four funky-patterned long-sleeve shirts, and two strappy tanks with extra support.

"No reason to look ugly when pregnant anymore," she says, without looking at me.

"Thank you," I tell her, resisting the urge to give her a hug that might make her regret her kind gesture.

She is dressed as though ready to go to a nightclub. She met someone who looks promising. A financier, originally from Hong Kong, who is recently widowed. She thinks that they understand each other better because the cultural differences aren't so great. She told me this as she wriggled into her skintight designer denim and fastened her chandelier earrings to her earlobes. Her cheeks were flushed and her eyes sparkled, and I realized that as energetic as she has always been, she's never looked so alive.

"Not bad," she says as she sets the box down in a corner of the living room. "Kind of dark."

"It's just the time of day," I say defensively. "You should see it in the mornings. The light comes streaming in those windows." I point across the doorway to the kitchen windows.

Ahma wanders around the living room. She sees the picture of Mr. Park and his wife on the shelf above the fireplace.

"He married American lady?" she asks.

"Yes."

"He look like your father. Handsome," she says. "But lady look cheap."

I don't tell her that her husband had an affair with the cheap-looking lady.

"It was just the style back then. Everyone used to dress like that."

"Not me," she says. "I was back then, too."

I am struck by the truth of her words, a truth that she doesn't realize. She *was* back then. My parents were married at the time the picture was taken. Had the affair already started? Was Mr. Park's wife going to meet my father later, in that same tube top and miniskirt? It is odd to contemplate. I am grateful now to Mr. Park for leaving the words in my father's notebook untranslated, for just telling me enough to understand him better. It is easier for me to remember what I want about my father without knowing everything. Unlike my mother, who now knows too much.

She must have found his notebook and read it after he died. That would explain why she decided to throw all his things away, why she stopped grieving so abruptly, why she was so determined to *move on* with her life. She may have had her doubts and suspicions about their marriage, but she couldn't have known for certain. Not knowing made it possible for her to continue living their lie.

But after reading his notebook, she could no longer deny the truth. She could throw it away in the garbage with all his other belongings, but she could not unread his words. He had betrayed her. But even worse, for all those years, she had deceived herself. Perhaps that was what hurt the most.

She does not know that I know, and I will not tell her. What would be gained? I want to spare her more shame and hurt, both of which would be compounded by my knowledge. She has changed so much this year. Would she have been able to do that if, every time she looked at me, she was reminded of my father's betrayal? The past would have lurked like a troll under a bridge, blocking the path to her future.

I offer her some tea, but she refuses.

"I have to meet Wayne," she says. Wayne is the financier from Hong Kong, the reason for her sparkling eyes and flushed cheeks. "He take me to dinner. Nice restaurant."

"Not La Chemise," I groan.

"Not French restaurant. Japanese. Best sushi. Very fresh. Famous chef." She looks at me, and a shadow of concern darkens her face. "You want to come?"

I shake my head. "No. What would Wayne think?"

"He don't care. He Chinese!" she says, meaning that he understands that family is part of the deal.

"No. I'm just going to relax and watch some TV and unpack."

"Take lots of rest. Don't let feet get too fat."

"I will. I won't. Have fun."

She gives me a peck on the cheek. I wave to her as she pulls her car out of the driveway.

I make myself a cup of green tea. I will have to replenish Mr. Park's stash before he gets back. His tea comes curled in balls that slowly unfurl as they steep. It doesn't have the bitter edge of the cheap green tea that I buy.

I drink my tea and watch the daylight fade over the hills until there is nothing but a hazy orange across the skies. I get up and start to unpack the last boxes. I want to be ready when the baby comes, and there is still so much I need. Janine promised me a baby shower, despite my protestations. She knows me well enough to realize that even though a shower will embarrass me and make me feel uncomfortable, I will love every minute of it.

My feet hurt so I sit in the leather chair and turn the television channel to a news program about climate change. Melting glaciers, hurricanes, wildfires. I watch patterns of red and green on an illustrated map, and the red rapidly spreading across the screen. I see pictures of a tourist village in Switzerland twenty years ago, a winter wonderland for vacationing Europeans. Pictures of the same village today show dusty brown shops and empty streets. In only a hundred years. Fifty years. Twenty years. This is what it means to live, to build a life, to populate a planet. This is what it means to be part of the universe, to be interconnected. The cumulative effects of billions of people over time.

After I found out I was pregnant, I applied to the master of accountancy program at the university. If I'm going to support a family, I'm going to need a better-paying job. It was a decision that I made alone, and one that I finally shared last week with Ahma and Janine. My mother seemed pleased but didn't say anything.

"But aren't you too . . . old?" Janine asked. "By the time you graduate, you'll be . . ."

"The same age I would be if I didn't do it."

There was no point in waiting for the perfect time, the perfect person, the perfect opportunity. I understand better now that there is no choice to opt out of a life. It is about more than simply seizing the day.

It is about the accumulation of days, the way each moment, each decision, connects to the next, how just the sheer number of decisions, no matter how small or seemingly inconsequential, can shape your life, can *be* your life. The incrementalism of existence, the winds that eventually create canyons. The years pass, so stealthily, whether you choose to pay attention or not, whether you are ready or not. You have more need of time than it has of you.

It seems so important now to be ever vigilant, ever mindful, of how I spend my days. I stand and stretch, arching my back. I instinctively rub my stomach, even though I have not yet felt any movement. My doctor promises me that I will, any day now.

I empty one more box, the one that Ahma carried in for me. Inside are papers—my passport, old bills, bank statements. Hidden carefully underneath everything is the large yellow envelope. I open it. Inside is Appa's notebook. I look at the characters, my father's handwriting. I wonder whether my father regretted his life, and if so, what parts of it. Did he regret his affair? Marrying Ahma? Having me? It is the last question that troubles me the most. I know that it would have been easier for him to leave my mother if it hadn't been for me.

But I am not to blame for his unhappiness. It was his love for Crystal River that, like a weed, wound its way through our family and stifled the passion that my father must have felt at one time for my mother, strangling the bond that could have grown between them and that was necessary for our family to flourish. It was his love for the woman he could not have that made him unable to love the woman he married.

This thought fills me with sadness. My sympathies had been only with my mother, who loved a man who refused to love her back. But now I understand that my father, too, deserved sympathy, because he was the one who could not be with his true love, and so he was the one who suffered the most.

CHAPTER

TWENTY-ONE

April 5, 2010

Last night, I had the most beautiful dream. Shirley appeared before me in a cloud of white and gray. She beckoned to me with arms that became beautiful swan's wings. I reached out to her and felt one of her wings flutter across my hands. They felt so soft, like powder sprinkled on my skin. When I awoke, I noticed the skin on the back of my hands had become mottled with brown spots. I didn't dare show them to my wife.

My longing for Shirley became so strong then. That is when I felt the pain in my chest. It felt as though my heart were breaking. But I know that is silly. If a heart could actually break like a china cup, mine would have shattered many years ago.

I feel it will be time soon. It will be time for me to come home. This is what she whispered to me before she touched me. This is what I eagerly await. This is what I wish so hard to believe.

ACKNOWLEDGMENTS

I would not have had the opportunities in my life if it weren't for the sacrifices made by my parents, Yeun Soo and Mi Wha Kim, to whom I owe a debt of gratitude. They taught me so much over the years, including what makes a good marriage, how to live with humor, compassion, and honesty, and the importance of taking ownership of one's life.

This book is in many ways a collective effort. I thank my agent, Priya Doraswamy of Lotus Lane Literary, for encouragement, patience, and guidance every step of the way—and for finding the perfect home for this book at Lake Union. I thank Erin Calligan Mooney and Danielle Marshall for taking a chance on an unknown author and for managing the book and the entire process with such care and attention, David Downing for diligent editing and asking the tough questions needed to strengthen the story, Nicole Burns-Ascue for shepherding the production process, Bill Siever and Sylvia M. for fine-tuning edits, and the rest of the Lake Union team for their work in bringing this book into the hands of readers.

I am extremely fortunate to have a generous, understanding, and loving family willing to be my support network and sounding board. Many thanks to Mina, for reading drafts, sharing my angst, and bestowing your youthful, wise counsel—the story and I are both better for it; to Amelia, for your dry wit, clever insights, and the irresistible dumplings and baked goods that brightened many dreary days and made writing infinitely more enjoyable; and, of course, to my husband, Seth, for the dinners, much appreciated cups of chicory coffee, hugs, morning runs, long walks, and so much more—all of which lifted my spirits and made it possible for me to find the time, space, and energy to write. I love and appreciate you three so much. This book is as much yours as it is mine.

BOOK CLUB QUESTIONS

1. How does Alice change over the course of the book?

2. Alice observes that her mother changes after her father's death. How does her mother change? How do her mother's changes compare with the changes Alice experiences?

3. Alice feels conflicted when she gives her father's notebook to Mr. Park to translate. What eventually makes her do it? Have you ever experienced a similar situation where you had to share a personal secret with someone who was not a trusted friend or confidante?

4. What do you think leads Mr. Park to suspect that Shirley is Crystal River?

5. How would you describe the relationship between Alice and her mother?

6. Alice and Janine have been friends for decades. What keeps their friendship strong? Do you have a childhood friend whom you have remained close with over the years?

7. The book is clearly set in Southern California. Could the story have taken place elsewhere? Are there aspects of the story that make it distinctively Southern Californian?

8. What type of place is Restin? What draws Alice to the place?

9. The characters each view themselves in a specific way. Does their self-image reflect reality?

10. What are your feelings toward Alice's father? Are you sympathetic? Disdainful?

11. Alice muses that her life did not turn out the way she expected. What do you think she expected her life to be like?

12. What keeps Alice and her mother from being openly honest with each other? Do the secrets they keep from each other enhance or diminish their relationship?

ABOUT THE AUTHOR

Photo © 2020 Mina Burns

Nancy Kim is the author of several nonfiction books and a novel, *Chinhominey's Secret*. She was born in Seoul, Korea, and grew up in Southern California. She received her BA and JD from the University of California, Berkeley, and an LLM from the University of California, Los Angeles. She is a law professor and an expert on contracts, and she has lectured at universities around the world. She currently lives in Southern California with her husband and two daughters.